THERE ARE TWO KINDS OF PEOPLE.

"Haunted houses aren't exactly rare," she mused. "Which means there has to be something somewhere that could help."

I wrinkled my nose at her. "Help?"

Dropping her spoon, Liv raised her eyebrows at me. "Well, yeah. Why else would we be doing all this research about a haunted house if we weren't gonna, you know, de-haunt it?"

"Ohhhh, Liv," I sighed. "Ohhhhhhlivia." And she picked up a stray sprinkle from the table and flicked it at me.

I dodged, giggling, but still said, "We can't fix it. We can just, you know, understand what it is. Know what we're up against and how to best keep ourselves non-ghost-smacked for the rest of the summer. I'm not about to go full-on Ghostbuster at Live Oak House."

RUBY & OLIVIA

OTHER BOOKS YOU MAY ENJOY

Ruby & Olivia

Rachel Hawkins

PUFFIN BOOKS

PUFFIN BOOKS
An imprint of Penguin Random House LLC
375 Hudson Street
New York, New York 10014

First published in the United States of America by G. P. Putnam's Sons,
an imprint of Penguin Random House LLC, 2017
Published by Puffin Books, an imprint of Penguin Random House LLC, 2018

THE LIBRARY OF CONGRESS HAS CATALOGED THE G. P. PUTNAM'S SONS EDITION AS FOLLOWS:
Names: Hawkins, Rachel, 1979– author.
Title: Ruby & Olivia / Rachel Hawkins.
Other titles: Ruby and Olivia
Description: New York, NY : G. P. Putnam's Sons, [2017] | Summary: Quiet
Olivia and brash Ruby, her twin sister's best friend, paired at a summer
camp for troublemakers to work in an old mansion, must really unite when
strange things begin to happen.
Identifiers: LCCN 2017004686 | ISBN 9780399169618 (hardcover)
Subjects: | CYAC: Haunted houses—Fiction. | Camps—Fiction. |
Friendship—Fiction. | Conduct of life—Fiction. | Sisters—Fiction. |
Twins—Fiction.
Classification: LCC PZ7.H313525 Rub 2017 | DDC [Fic]—dc23
LC record available at https://lccn.loc.gov/2017004686

Puffin Books ISBN 9780147512918

Design by Jaclyn Reyes

Printed in the United States of America

1 3 5 7 9 10 8 6 4 2

For Will

PROLOGUE

RubyToozday: So I think we should definitely write it all down. Everything that happened.

OliviaAnneWillingham: That . . . does not seem like a good idea.

RubyToozday: Why not?

OliviaAnneWillingham: If you can't get why putting down *in writing* that we destroyed a town landmark is not a good idea, I don't know what to tell you.

RubyToozday: But we didn't destroy it! Not on PURPOSE. That's the whole point of this! Making sure that if it ever DOES come out, what really happened, we've gotten the FACTS STRAIGHT.

RubyToozday: Why do you hate facts?

OliviaAnneWillingham: Fine, you can write it down if you want, but I want it to be really clear that none of this was my fault.

RubyToozday: That is a lie.

RubyToozday: We're documenting this for science, Liv.

RubyToozday: There's no lying in science.

OliviaAnneWillingham: Ugh. Okay, but I'll do my part on my own, okay?

RubyToozday: That seems fair and also scientific.

CHAPTER 1

OLIVIA

None of this was actually my fault.

I wouldn't have even been at Live Oak House this summer if it hadn't been for my sister, Emma. My *twin* sister, Emma.

Sometimes it's weird to look at someone who shares my face but couldn't be more different from me if she'd been born on another planet. Mom says that it's because we're twins that we're so different, that we're always trying to make it easier for people to tell us apart. I don't think that's true for me, but it definitely is for Em.

We're what's known as mirror twins. We're completely identical, but in reverse. The little brown freckle near my left temple? It's there on Em's face, too, but on the right. She's left-handed, I'm right-handed.

When we were little, our mom made sure we matched all the time—same little dresses, same hairstyles, all of that. It was only last year that Emma rebelled and started wearing what she wanted. I'd never minded matching, but if Emma didn't want to do it anymore, I told myself I needed to be okay with that. Then on that Saturday, the day that screwed everything up, Emma came out of her room dressed the same as me for the first time in ages. It was an accident.

I hadn't told Em what I was wearing that day, and she hadn't come into my room to see me before she got dressed. It happened that way sometimes, an easy thing to do since we still had a lot of the same clothes. We'd both worn jeans and the pale blue blouses Mom had bought us a few weeks before. I liked the blouse because of the little flowers embroidered around the neck, and Emma's favorite color was blue.

Honestly, I'd expected Emma to ask me to change, but that day, she'd just shrugged it off. "One more time won't hurt," she'd said, and I'd been happy about that.

Things had been . . . weird with me and Em for nearly a year by then. Not in a big way, really, but if I was pretty content being *EmmaandOlivia*, all one word like that, I could tell Emma wasn't. It had started in little ways—wanting her own room, her own clothes—but turned into wanting her own friends and her own interests, people and hobbies that it seemed like she picked because she *knew* I wouldn't like them.

Like Camp Kethaway.

Camp Kethaway had been Emma's obsession for months, ever since she'd seen a stack of brochures in the guidance counselor's office. It was your traditional summer camp—canoeing, arts and crafts, s'mores, all that, which had sounded like a nightmare to me.

Staying in the woods with a bunch of people you don't know? Forced camaraderie? No, thank you.

I'd told Emma right from the beginning to count me out of her Camp Kethaway plans, and I think part of me had assumed she'd scrap the idea. We were kind of a package deal, me and Em, so surely if *I* didn't want to do it, she wouldn't, either.

But no, Emma had just gone on planning for camp, begging Mom and Dad until they relented. She was scheduled to leave just a few days after the lipstick thing.

We were going shopping with Mom, something neither of us really liked all that much, except I got to spend time in the bookstore, and Mom let Em go to the Sephora even though we weren't allowed to wear makeup. Emma always said the trips to Sephora were "scouting missions," that she was learning what kind of makeup she liked so that when she *was* allowed to wear more than slightly tinted ChapStick—on our fourteenth birthday, according to Mom—she'd be prepared.

The lipstick she took wasn't even a color she liked. It was too bright, almost hot pink, and Emma didn't like pink. *I* did, though, and maybe that's why Mom believed me.

I can still remember standing there at the front of the store with Mom and Em, the security guard, and the cashier with the pretty blond hair, a bright streak of purple over one eye. Mom's arms were folded over her chest, and her face was pinched and tight, white lines edging her lips. Mom had never been this mad at us before, but then we'd never given her any reason to be before that day.

And really, I can't blame Em. Em didn't point a finger at me and say, "It wasn't me, it was Olivia." *I* was the one who said, "I did it. I took the lipstick."

Even now, I don't know exactly why I said that. Maybe it was because I'd known that Mom would punish Emma by canceling her summer camp. Maybe I thought Emma would think I was cool for owning up to a crime I didn't commit.

And maybe—just *maybe*—when I said I'd been the one to take the makeup, I thought Emma would fess up even though she had to know that would mean the end of Camp Kethaway.

Maybe I thought Em would pick me over camp.

But she just bit her lip while Mom looked back and forth between us.

"Livvy, this is just . . . It's so unlike you," Mom finally said, and I saw Emma flinch a little bit. I couldn't blame her. Was Mom saying shoplifting *was* like Emma? Sure, she'd been going through some changes lately, switching out new crowds of friends every few weeks, it seemed like, but she'd never really been in serious trouble before.

I just shrugged and said, "I wanted to be different."

I still don't know if Mom actually believed me, but she sighed and nodded, and that was that. Obviously no one wanted to press charges against a twelve-year-old, but that didn't mean I was getting off scot-free.

Camp Chrysalis had been a thing in Chester's Gap forever, and I remembered past summers, seeing kids in brightly colored T-shirts picking up trash at the park, cleaning up the area around the country club pool. Some years there were only four or five kids. Sometimes there were nearly twenty. The camp wasn't just for our town anymore, but had opened up to the nearby towns in the tri-county area as a "positive redirection" for kids who'd screwed up. It had never in a million years occurred to me that I'd end up there. I'd thought with Emma away at Camp Kethaway, I'd be spending my own summer reading, maybe going to the pool.

Camp Chrysalis met at the town rec center not too far from our neighborhood, and as Mom drove up that first morning, I sat in the passenger seat, fingers laced together, hands in my lap. A whole summer of picking up trash. Of people *seeing* me pick up trash. For something I didn't even do.

"Little different from yesterday, huh?" Mom asked lightly as we pulled into the circular drive in front of the center. I'd always hated this building, all squat and square and brick, with columns painted like crayons. Somehow all those bright colors against the dingy brick just made it worse.

"Definitely wish I were at Em's camp instead," I answered.

We'd dropped Emma off the day before, and when I'd seen the way she smiled at the little circle of cabins and the brightly colored banner flapping in the wind at the top of a flagpole in the middle of that circle, I'd felt . . . okay. It was nice that Emma was going to get to do this thing she really wanted to do. I could still have a good summer, even with Camp Chrysalis.

The feeling of okay popped like a soap bubble as we walked into the rec center.

Mom put her hand on my shoulder, squeezing a little. "It'll be fine," she said, and I nodded, my mouth dry.

Leaning down, Mom looked into my face, her brows drawn

together, and I saw it again, that same look she'd been giving me since the Lipstick Incident—like the truth of it was there if only she could see it. Mom knew me, after all. And she knew Em. And I think she knew who'd really taken that lipstick, but since I wasn't cracking, there was nothing she could do about it.

Finally, she sighed and straightened up.

"Okay, let's get you signed in."

The camp was meeting in the gym, and we walked down a carpeted hallway in that direction, stopping at the big double doors and glancing inside. Three kids were already there— Garrett McNamara, a blond boy a year ahead of me who I'd seen at school; a smaller kid named Wesley, who was in my grade; and then, coming through the doors on the other side of the gym, a very familiar face, and one I really, really didn't want to see.

Ruby Kaye.

CHAPTER 2

RUBY

Liv got sent to Camp Chrysalis because of something her sister did that she—totally stupidly, I should add—took the blame for.

Me?

I actually did the thing.

It's a long story, but it involved getting on the wrong bus on our school field trip to the art museum, then making a deal with this kid from a different school to switch pranks. You know, I'd do a prank at his school, he'd do one at mine, and we'd never get caught because no one is looking for a suspect outside the school, right? *Such* a good idea.

I'd gotten it from this old movie I'd watched with my grammy once. I used to go to her house after school every day until my mom was done with work, and one of mine and Grammy's favorite things to do was watch old movies together. Grammy wasn't very old, and most of the movies she liked had been made before she was born, but she was a sucker for anything black-and-white and spooky. In the movie, a guy gets on a train, and he and a stranger learn they each have a person in their life they wish they could murder. They decide to murder the other person's person, figuring that that way, no one can connect them to the crimes. Obviously, that was way more intense than what I wanted to do, but when I got on that wrong bus, I realized it was the perfect opportunity for something *like* that, at least.

I think Grammy would've laughed.

But the other kid, Harrison, was a total weenie and didn't do the prank at Yardley Middle School, while I *did* do the prank at Chester's Gap Junior High. While I didn't think it was *that* big of a deal (like, you can vacuum up glitter, even *that much* glitter, I'm pretty sure), the "vandalism" got me in serious trouble, and my punishment included Camp Chrysalis.

Honestly, I would rather have been suspended, and I didn't think it was fair that *my* school got to punish me for something that happened at *another* school, but then my mom said she'd add to my punishment if I kept complaining (no Xbox until my time with Camp Chrysalis was up), and no one needed that. So off to camp I went.

We met at the rec center gym on a really pretty June day, the kind of day when I should've been riding my bike or asking Mom to take me to the little park on the edge of town for a picnic and Frisbee.

Okay, so I'd never had a picnic or played Frisbee with my mom in my life, but that's not the point. The point is that there were a million things I could've been doing that were *not* going up to the rec center to do who knew what with Camp Chrysalis.

"They could be a cult, you know," I told Mom as we walked

through the blue double doors leading from the back parking lot. The air smelled like bleach and floor polish and that faintly sweaty smell that hangs around every gym, or at least all the ones I've been in. "We could end up doing some really weird stuff, Mom, and I might shave my head and change my name to Starflower. Do you want a daughter named Starflower?"

Mom sighed, and it was the bad kind, something I always thought of as an "H Sigh." It sounded kind of like "Heeeeeeeehhhhhhh," and she used it only when she was annoyed with me.

Since around fourth grade, I'd gotten really familiar with the H Sigh.

"Maybe you should've thought of that before you were so destructive," Mom reminded me, and I frowned.

"Destructive? It was glitter! There's nothing destructive about *glitter*."

I might have gotten the H Sigh again then, but we were interrupted by Mrs. Freely. She worked for the Baptist church and had done a lot of substitute teaching when I was in elementary school. She also ran the camp, and while she was probably around my mom's age, I always thought she looked older. Maybe it was her hair, cut in one of those weird short styles that sticks up, but on purpose? Plus, it was an ash blond that made parts of it look gray. She was wearing elastic-waisted khaki capri pants and slip-on sneakers in the same hot pink as her T-shirt.

"Ruby, hiiiii!" she said, her smile nearly as big as the grinning smiley face printed on her tee. CAMP CHRYSALIS, the shirt blared. MAKING OUR LIVES BETTER ONE SMILE AT A TIME. Gross.

And then she handed me one of the shirts, and I started to think it was fine if I never played Xbox again so long as I didn't have to wear that creepy smiling head.

But Mom was looking at me, eyebrows raised, and I gave an H Sigh of my own, taking the shirt from Mrs. Freely. "Thank you," I said, and Mom lowered her eyebrows, relieved.

"We have got a busy day ahead, Miss Ruby!" Mrs. Freely said, and I remembered she was one of *those* grown-ups, the people who call kids "miss" and "mister," probably with a "buddy" thrown in every now and then.

She checked something off the clipboard she was holding, then moved on to her next victim, a kid I was pretty sure was named Wesley. He was in my grade, but the seventh grade had like five hundred kids in it, so it was hard to keep everyone straight.

"It's not going to be so bad," Mom said, leaning down a little closer to me. She smelled like green apple shampoo and the orange Tic Tacs she always had in her purse. "Hey, you might even make some friends."

"I have friends," I said, and Mom put an arm around me, giving me a little shake.

"Real friends, Rubes," she said. "People who can come over to the house."

Ugh. Like I needed a reminder that after Emma Willingham and I had stopped talking, my social life had been kind of limited. It's not that I didn't have friends—I totally did—just that I'd never really gotten all that close to anyone besides Emma. Between her and Grammy and, yes, the people I talked to online, I'd felt pretty complete on the friendship scale. But then Emma had gotten mad at me, Grammy had died, and all I was left with were DolphinWhisperer2005 and SailorMoonXX.

Stepping out of her embrace, I looked up at her. I wasn't going to have to do that for much longer—I was only a couple of inches shorter than Mom now, and since my dad had been tall, I had high hopes of towering over Mom by eighth grade.

"Internet friends *are* real friends," I replied, "and you do online dating."

This is a thing with me, that sometimes I say things before I've really *thought* about what will happen when I say them.

But Mom just laughed, shaking her head and pulling her purse up higher on her shoulder. "Okay, fair point," she said. "But I'm serious. You spend so much time yelling into that headset, and I'd like you to—"

"Yell at people in real life?" I offered.

Mom wrinkled her nose. "Not exactly. I just mean . . . Look, try to get some *good* out of this whole mess, okay? And Emma Willingham is here, see?" She nodded across the gym to the blond girl standing with her mom. "You and Emma used to be such good friends."

"That's not Emma," I said. "That's Olivia."

It was so obvious to me that I was surprised Mom had made the mistake. Emma wouldn't have been standing there with her head kind of down and her shoulders rolled forward, like she was trying to disappear into herself.

That was a total Olivia move.

I'd known the Willingham twins since I was really little, and used to be friends with both of them. Well, I always liked Emma more, but when we were younger, Olivia had been okay. It was only around fifth grade that she started to bug me, always seeming irritated when I was over at her house, glaring at me and Emma over the top of whatever book she was reading.

But then Emma and I had stopped hanging out last year, all because I said a certain boy who went to our school was cute.

Problem was, Emma liked that certain boy and apparently she thought me pointing out that he was cute meant that *I* liked him, which was *not true*. I was just . . . making an observation about the world around me.

So that had been the end of me and Emma hanging out, and now her sister was here, sentenced to the same summer punishment as me, which was maybe the weirdest thing ever. What on earth could Olivia Willingham have done to get sent to Camp Chrysalis? Forgotten to say please? Worn pink on Tuesdays instead of Wednesdays? Mom blinked at Olivia, clearly trying to figure out why the *good* twin was here. "Okay," she said slowly. "Then . . . maybe . . . you and Olivia could be friends again?"

I think that idea was even more horrifying than the pink T-shirt.

CHAPTER 3

OLIVIA

Walking up to the rec center may have reminded me just how much of a bummer my summer was going to be, but it was seeing Ruby Kaye standing there with her mom that brought home how Not Okay any of this was. I had enough trouble talking to strangers, but having to deal with someone I didn't like all summer, too? Someone who might turn these new people against me the same way she'd turned Emma against me?

Ruby and Emma had been friends since first grade—best friends, really—although in the past year or so, they'd had some kind of falling-out. I wasn't sure why, because Emma just sort of stopped talking about Ruby, and to be honest, I was so relieved she wouldn't be hanging around anymore that I didn't question it. All three of us were friends when we were littler, playing Barbies together, watching cartoons in our den. Ruby was always really good at coming up with stories for dress-up, I remembered. But then, around fifth grade, they tried to put my hand in warm water while I was sleeping that one time at Lindsey Green's sleepover, and I'd felt like it was starting to be Ruby and Emma plus *me* instead of me and Emma plus *Ruby*.

It was always supposed to be me and Emma plus *someone else*. We were literally a matched set, after all, and I didn't *want* to be the Plus Person.

Besides, Ruby was loud and always wore weird T-shirts. (The one she had on now was black with some kind of symbol on it that I didn't recognize—probably a video game thing. Ruby was super into all that stuff.) And she made Emma laugh in a way that I'd never been able to. She made everybody laugh, really, but I'd always thought it was obnoxious, the way she had a joke for everything. I'd sat through more classes than I could count where Ruby had gotten the whole class giggling and then we'd ended up with extra work as a punishment.

So I looked at her now across the gym and did my best not to scowl. She saw me looking and pushed her black hair behind her ears. There was a streak of blue in all the black now, just above one eye, and I wondered how she'd talked her mom into letting her do that.

"Oh, it's Ruby," Mom said faintly. Mom liked Ruby more than I did—that wasn't hard to do—but sometimes I thought she was relieved Ruby and Em weren't that close anymore, too. Chaos had a way of breaking out when Ruby was over.

"At least that's someone you know!" Mom continued, and I shrugged, not wanting to talk about it.

But Mom waved at Ruby's mom and started walking over that way.

"Beth!" she called, and Ruby's mom smiled, her face brightening.

"Hi, Connie," she said, reaching in for a quick hug. "Hey, Olivia."

"Hi, Ms. Kaye," I replied, and Ruby wiggled her fingers at my mom.

"Mrs. Willingham."

"So this is . . . interesting," Ruby's mom said, and my mom took a deep breath, squeezing my shoulder.

"That's one word for it," she replied, and I looked up at her, wishing I could will her to stop talking with my mind.

Ruby was watching her mom with the same intensity, and I studied her for a second, remembering the last time I'd really talked to her.

Not that it was that hard. In a lot of ways, the argument I'd had with Ruby at the end of sixth grade had been the beginning of things getting weird with me and Emma.

But I didn't want to think about that right then.

Luckily, at that moment, a guy and a girl walked over, both in the same bright pink T-shirt Mrs. Freely was wearing. The guy was blond, his hair sticking up in the front, while the girl had pretty red hair pulled up in a high ponytail, and they were both wearing name tags.

His said LEE. Hers said LEIGH. Mom laughed lightly and waved a hand at them. "Well, that might get confusing."

But Lee and Leigh just kept smiling. "It's easier to keep straight than you'd think!" Leigh said brightly, and Lee marked my name off his clipboard as Leigh handed me a shirt to match theirs.

As they walked off to greet another kid, Mom glanced down at me.

"You'll be okay," she told me, and I had that horrible soreness in my throat, my eyes stinging.

I was not going to cry. I was *not*.

Ruffling my hair, Mom leaned down and pressed a quick kiss to my temple. "See you at three," she said, and I nodded, taking a deep breath.

Three. That wasn't that far away. Just like a regular school day, and only three days a week.

I could do this.

There was a stack of gym mats on the floor, and I headed for those, sitting down with my new pink shirt clutched to my chest.

At least it was my favorite color? Even though that face on the front was creepy.

I unfolded the shirt, studying it. A smiley face was nothing new, but the smile was too wide, and smiley faces shouldn't have *teeth*. That's just disturbing.

Sighing, I put the shirt down.

Camp Chrysalis.

A place that everyone knew was for Bad Kids. I had never been a Bad Kid in my *life*. I was the one teachers always asked to watch the class when they had to step out of the room. I was the one whose clothespin was always on green when I was little. Even Emma had never really been a Bad Kid, and she'd *still* heard, "I wish you were more like your sister." I wonder if that bugged her.

The whole rec center gym smelled like feet and floor polish, and the mat I was sitting on stuck to the back of my legs. Overhead, giant fans whirred on the ceiling, but they didn't do much to cool the place down, and I thought of Emma, off at camp. Of how nice the camp looked, and of that big, shining lake we'd seen as we'd driven in. Was she swimming in that lake right now?

Ruby Kaye was still standing by the door, talking to her mom, and I could see her wrinkle her nose when she got her T-shirt. Mrs. Freely was with them, grinning just as big as the Camp Chrysalis smiley face, and she gave Ruby a pat on the shoulder, then turned, pointing at . . . me.

Please don't sit here, please don't sit here, I silently prayed, and from the narrowing of Ruby's eyes, I had a feeling she could sense what I was thinking.

And apparently agreed, since she turned, hugged her mom quickly, and then went to the opposite side of the mat I was sitting on.

There was a boy on that side who I had seen at school before but whose name I couldn't remember. He was probably older than us, and was certainly taller than the other boy already sitting on the mats. The tall boy's blond hair flopped over his forehead, and his basketball shorts had a hole in the hem. He sat down next to Ruby, and for a second, I thought she looked a little surprised. Her eyes sort of went wide and she got really still all of a sudden before drawing her knees up to her chest and wrapping her arms around them. I would've wondered what that was about, but then I reminded myself that I didn't care what Ruby Kaye thought or did, so I turned to watch the front of the room again.

Two more kids trickled in, but I didn't recognize either of them, and I guessed they must be from other towns, other counties, even. They were both boys, too, although just before nine, another girl came in. I watched her, kind of hoping she'd sit next to me—she was wearing a ribbon around her braid that matched her mint-green polo shirt, so clearly we could be friends—but she sat right in the middle, her shoulders hunched forward in a very clear "don't talk to me" posture.

Mrs. Freely was still standing next to the door with her clipboard, her helpers next to her, and she checked her watch before giving a firm nod and walking over to stand in front of us.

"Good morning, campers!" she trilled, like we were at a real camp, not . . . whatever this was. I glanced around and saw that there were only seven of us: me, Ruby, that blond boy from school, the Black girl in green, the two boys who came in together, and Wesley. He had longish hair and was currently combing it over his face, hiding his eyes.

Great.

"I know you're not used to being up this bright and early in the summertime," Mrs. Freely went on, grinning, "but we like to get an early start here at Camp Chrysalis, don't we, guys?!"

Her two helpers, Lee and Leigh, both responded with

"Yeah!"—so in sync that it was clearly rehearsed—and from the other side of the mat, I heard Ruby snort.

Mrs. Freely heard it, too, and while her smile didn't fade, her eyes seemed to go a bit harder as she looked at Ruby.

"It can take a while for attitudes to change," she said, "but I promise, by the time you leave Camp Chrysalis, you'll feel like a whole new person! You're going to learn so much about yourselves this summer through the spirit of service. But first! *I* want to learn about *you*! Everybody on your feet!"

The blond boy next to Ruby dropped his forehead onto his folded arms, and the other girl rolled her eyes. I couldn't see Wesley's expression behind all his hair, but I could sense the other two boys fidgeting behind me.

I rose to my feet first, and then, slowly, everyone did the same. Ruby was the last to stand up, and as she did, Mrs. Freely gestured for us all to form a sort of semicircle. Then, still grinning, she pointed at herself. "I'm Mrs. Freely, and I'm friendly."

Wait, we weren't going to have to— "I'm Lee!" Lee enthused. "And I'm laid-back." He punctuated that with a little wave of his thumb and pinky, like he was a surfer dude in some dumb movie, and I could feel my face getting hotter and hotter.

"I'm Leigh," Leigh said, stepping forward and pushing her hair off her shoulders. "And I'm loquacious!"

We all stared at her for a second, and her smile dipped the littlest bit. "SAT prep," she muttered. "It means 'talkative'?"

"And it's an excellent word, Leigh," Mrs. Freely assured her. "Now, Olivia, your turn!"

Eyes turned to me, and I swallowed hard, my voice thin when I said, "I'm Olivia, and I'm . . . organized."

I could hear smothered giggles from around the circle, but I kept my eyes on the tips of my shoes. *This* is exactly the kind of thing I'd wanted to avoid, why I didn't want to go to camp with Em in the first place.

"I'm Ruby," Ruby piped up from across the circle, even though the redheaded boy was next to me and technically should've gone next. "And I am *rarin'* to get started!"

This time the giggles were louder, and when I looked up, I realized Ruby was doing the full finger-guns thing at Mrs. Freely.

Looked like Ruby hadn't changed at all.

"I'm Susanna," said the only other girl here, the one in green I'd noticed when she first came in. "And I'm super-bummed to be here."

Mrs. Freely frowned. "Now, Susanna, that's really not the attitude—"

"I'm Dalton," the redheaded boy next to me chimed in. "And I'm dead inside."

"I'm Garrett." That was the tall blond boy I'd seen sit next to Ruby. "I'm going to throw up."

By now, Mrs. Freely had both hands on her hips and was glaring around the semicircle, so the other boy I didn't recognize, the dark-haired one, hurriedly said, "I'm Michael. I'm . . . mostly okay with being here?"

We all looked at Wesley, the last kid not to have said anything, and he just stood there, his face still covered by his hair.

He might have muttered something, but it was hard to tell, and I think Mrs. Freely was ready to move on at this point.

Gesturing for us to sit, she said, "Well, now at least we all know each other's names, and . . . some of the challenges we'll be facing this summer. And speaking of this summer! Let's tell y'all about what we'll be doing, because it's pretty special!"

Leigh stepped forward, her smile as bright as Mrs. Freely's, if slightly less clenched. "Camp Chrysalis is all about helping to better our community," she started. "Sometimes that means picking up trash at Kensley Park, or planting flowers downtown. But this year, we have a project that is going to *blow. Y'all. Away.*"

She said it so dramatically, her hands outspread, her blue eyes wide, that I felt bad that we were all staring at her, so I sat up a little straighter, putting myself in the best position to be blown away.

Leigh cleared her throat as it became clear that my fellow campers were definitely *not* excited. Ruby was picking at the toe of her shoe, Garrett was making that hole in the hem of his shorts bigger, and Wesley . . . well, he was still hiding behind his hair, so who knew what he was doing? Susanna was watching Leigh, at least, but her eyes seemed about a million miles away.

Leigh soldiered on. "How many of you have ever heard of Live Oak House?"

I raised my hand and saw Ruby's hand go up, too, along with Wesley's and Garrett's. Dalton raised his hand, too, if sort of flopping it up for a second could be called raising his hand. I was actually surprised anyone outside of Chester's Gap had heard of the place. It was a big house on the edge of town, abandoned for ages, and there were all sorts of weird rumors about it. The guy who had lived there had kept to himself, never getting married or having kids, and hardly ever coming into town. I hadn't really paid attention to the house because I'd never had any reason to go past it, and scary stuff wasn't really my thing anyway.

"Well," Leigh went on, "then you may know that Live Oak House is one of the oldest houses in Chester's Gap, and certainly the biggest. It's been in the Wrexhall family since it was built in 1903, but sadly, the last Wrexhall, Mr. Matthew, died earlier this year."

I remembered that. It had been a big deal because Mr. Matthew (that's what everyone called him) had been over a hundred, but still living in that big old house on the edge of town, all by himself.

"Mr. Matthew never married," Leigh went on, "and his father, the man who built Live Oak House, Felix Wrexhall, hadn't had any other close family—" She paused, looking back over her shoulder at Mrs. Freely. "You were a cousin, right?"

Mrs. Freely waved that off. "So distant I couldn't even track it, but apparently so."

Leigh turned back to us. "Anyway, in his will, Mr. Matthew left the house to the town of Chester's Gap. And the town council has decided to restore Live Oak House to its former glory so that it can be a museum or maybe an event space. Once y'all see it, I think you'll understand what a special place it is, and why people would want to hold weddings there, or fancy parties. It is *really* something. And!" She paused for effect, tucking her dark hair behind her ears. "That's going to start with *you*!"

That expectant look again, with the spread hands and the big eyes, and honestly, I was starting to feel a little sorry for her.

She glanced over at Lee, and he stepped forward, clapping his hands so loudly, we all kind of jumped.

"This is a unique opportunity for you to contribute to this town," he said, fixing us with that same bright smile Leigh and Mrs. Freely employed. I wondered if that was part of their training, learning to do that smile. "Now of course, they'll be bringing in professionals to do the big stuff, but the journey to a restored Live Oak House starts with us! Every day, we'll be going up to the house and cleaning some of the stuff inside. You'll even be responsible for cataloging some of the really unique pieces the Wrexhall family accumulated over the years. And once the house is all fixed up, every time you go to a wedding or a party out there, you'll be able to say, 'I helped make this happen!'"

I could tell that none of my fellow campers were all that impressed with that idea, but I found myself cheering up a little bit. Picking up trash would've been boring (and gross), but helping fix up an old house? Making it pretty and shiny again? That *did* feel like doing something positive, and I could get behind that. Plus, I liked the idea of going through all the neat old things that might be in Live Oak House. Mom, Emma, and I always watched those shows on HGTV where people went to flea markets and fixed up old furniture, turning it into something interesting and beautiful, and Emma had even begged Mom to take us to a flea market back in the spring so she could find some stuff for her room. She'd ended up with a wicker chair she'd painted yellow, and a really weird lamp that looked like a guitar.

Would she have liked Camp Chrysalis after all? I wondered. Lee stepped back, and Mrs. Freely took his place. "Every day, we'll be heading out to the house from here around this time. The camp will provide drinks and snacks, and we'll be back by two. From two to three, you can work on your Responsibility Journal, and at three, you get to head home!"

Responsibility Journal? I wasn't sure I liked the sound of it, and from the looks on my fellow campers' faces, they didn't, either. Susanna tucked her chin down, eyebrows drawing together, and from behind me, I thought I heard one of the boys I didn't know mutter a bad word.

Mrs. Freely was still talking, mostly about how we'd be split into groups once we got to the house, and I tried to pay attention, keeping my eyes trained on her face, hoping my own face looked eager and interested, like it was beaming out, *I didn't actually do a bad thing! But I am here to learn!* Mrs. Freely could feel all my exclamation points, right?

"Now, if everyone will come up here, we can start our day with song, then load up into the van."

My face fell, and any *I'm innocent!* in my expression gave way to, *Song?* We slowly got up from the mat, all seven of us shuffling our feet, sneakers squeaking on the floor as we made a sort of loose circle, Mrs. Freely pointing at where we should each stand. Lee and Leigh were on either side of her, and she took their hands. I was on Lee's other side, so I took his hand, and then looked over to see that Ruby Kaye was on my other side.

We stared at each other for a moment, and then with a sigh that ruffled her bangs, she took my hand.

CHAPTER 4

RUBY

We're not talking about the song we sang.

It's so embarrassing that to remember it now would cause me to spontaneously combust, but know that the word *friends* was repeated like a thousand times, and there might have been an attempt at swaying from Mrs. Freely and the Lee(igh)s.

Luckily, the van ride out to the house didn't require any kind of musical performance. It was a smallish van with three bench seats, room for three people on each one. Lee drove, Mrs. Freely in the passenger seat next to him, and Garrett McNamara sat on the bench behind her.

Garrett, the boy that Emma had liked, the boy I very much did *not* like, no matter what she said. Would Olivia tell Emma that Garrett was in the camp, too?

Probably.

Sighing, I picked the very back bench with two of the boys, hoping that since they clearly knew each other, they wouldn't talk to me.

I actually liked talking to people most of the time—I did it too much, probably—but I wasn't in the mood for conversation. And it turned out to be a smart decision, sitting with them, because just as I'd thought, they ignored me and muttered to each other.

Olivia Willingham sat on the second bench next to the other girl and Leigh. I looked at the back of her blond head, wondering why on earth she was here. Emma? That I could totally see. I'd really liked Emma, and she'd probably been the closest thing to a best friend I'd had before our stupid fight, but this whole past year, she'd been really weird. Like she was trying to figure out who she wanted to be, and every time she changed her mind, she changed her friends. It had to have bugged Olivia, but it's not like we'd ever talked about it, and the last time I'd seen her, she'd called me "weird" and said I was "going to get Emma into trouble."

Of course, Emma and I *had* been trying to sneak out that night, daring each other to run from Emma and Olivia's house to the front of their neighborhood where there was this little foun-tain set up by the big brick sign welcoming people to the Copper Ridge subdivision. It hadn't been far. I remembered that we could actually see the glow from the up-lights focused on the sign from Emma's window. We were just going to run to it, dip our fingers in the fountain, and run back. I can't even really remember *why* now except that we were bored, and it seemed like fun.

We'd opened the window when Olivia had appeared in the door in her oversize T-shirt and pajama pants that had little hedgehogs on them, her blond hair tangled around her face.

She'd glared at us and said all that about being weird and

trouble and whatever, and Emma had told her she was being a baby, and maybe I'd said something along the lines of, like, "Hi, if we wanted your input on this, we would have invited you," and that had really been the last time I'd talked to Olivia.

Just a few months later, the Garrett Incident happened, and then both the Willingham twins were out of my life.

I really wouldn't have minded if Emma had been here at Camp Chrysalis—I still thought there was a chance we could be friends again, maybe. But Olivia?

I snorted and settled back in my seat.

I spent most of the ride staring out the window, trying not to breathe in any Boy Smell. I'd begun to realize that not *all* boys smelled like socks, but these two definitely did, and I sighed, wishing we'd been allowed to bring our phones. But no, they were all stashed away in the lockers back at the rec center, along with the shirts we'd worn today and our dignity.

Live Oak House wasn't all that far out, but it was far enough that the drive made me kind of sleepy, and by the time the van rattled up the turnoff for the house, I had to sort of shake myself to wake up.

"Isn't it something?" Mrs. Freely said, turning in her seat to face us with that same creepy smile on her face.

It was indeed . . . something.

The van stopped on a dirt road at the base of a slight rise, and on the top of the rise was a house.

Okay, so calling that place a house is like calling a Ferrari a *car* or Halo a *video game*. Technically true, but it doesn't really describe the thing.

Live Oak House was bigger than any house I'd ever seen. We have a lot of fake-plantation-looking houses in the South, but this was nothing like that. It was all steep roofs and sharp points, and my drowsy brain actually thought, *Like a house with teeth.*

Which was stupid.

But there was no getting around the fact that even in the bright daylight, under blue skies, the house seemed sinister and dark, making its own shadows across the lawn. Out front, there was one massive oak tree with wide leaves rustling in the slight breeze.

Behind the house, the hill sloped down again into a bunch of trees, but the mansion took up most of the space, looking sort of like an overgrown dollhouse. It had been painted cream at one point, with pretty maroon trim, but even from the van I could see that the paint was peeling, and there were patches of gray wood around the front door.

I moved closer to the window, looking up at the roof. There seemed to be another big tree really close to the house, but in the back, its leaves spreading out over the highest peak of the roof like an umbrella. Tilting my head, I tried to get a better look, wanting to figure out where that tree was because it really *looked* like it was coming out of the house.

"This place is creepy," I muttered, and one of the boys next to me leaned over—ugh, maximum Boy Smell—to get closer to the window.

"For real," he replied.

Lee turned off the van, and Mrs. Freely hopped out, opening the doors so we could all file onto the dirt road. There was no drive leading up to the house, so I guessed this was the only place to park, and we all stood there, blinking in the bright sunshine as Mrs. Freely moved to the back of the van, throwing the double doors wide.

There were the plastic caddies I'd seen earlier, each one stocked with identical cleaners and rags, a roll of brown paper towels, and a box of plastic gloves. And shoved into each one was a spiral-bound notebook, all the same shade of hot pink as our shirts.

"Grab your caddy!" she trilled, and after a pause, we all moved to the back to grab one.

The cleaning supplies bumped against my leg as I made my way up the hill toward the house, and I squinted, wishing I'd thought to bring sunglasses.

Mrs. Freely walked up to the narrow steps leading to the front porch, pausing on the first one. Lee and Leigh fell in next to her, clipboards at the ready.

"Now," Mrs. Freely said, hands clasped in front of her like a general in hot pink, "I expect all of you to behave with respect once we're inside. Lee, Leigh, and I will be supervising as you begin today, and if we see even a little bit of horseplay, you will find yourself with a *much* less pleasant duty this summer."

I wondered what could possibly be less pleasant than dusting and making lists of old creepy stuff. Cleaning toilets at the rec center?

Studying Mrs. Freely's stern expression, I suddenly realized that I couldn't put toilet scrubbing past her. Yeah, no horseplay from me.

"Also," she went on, "because this is such a large house, we'll hardly be tackling all of it. Everything above the second floor is completely off-limits, and if you come to a closed door, do not open it. Lee, Leigh, and I have already been through, looking for places where we think you can all do the most good. Are you ready?"

I got the sense she wanted us to yell "READY!" all eager and excited, but no one said anything except for Olivia Willingham, and she kind of whispered, "Ready." If Olivia Willingham couldn't even pretend to get excited about this, Mrs. Freely was in some serious trouble.

Her smile barely faltered, though, and she turned to walk up the steps, Lee and Leigh close behind, the wood creaking slightly as they went. We all sort of lined up, and as Mrs. Freely stopped to unlock the front door, I turned to look back toward the lawn. The yard sloped down to the road where the van waited for us, the silver of the sunshade Lee had put in the windshield winking. I knew that only a few miles away was our town and the rec center, but standing there then, it was easy to believe we were in a whole different place. A whole different *time*, even. There was no sound from nearby traffic, no chatter of voices. Just our feet shuffling on the porch, the droning of bugs, and the occasional rustle of leaves.

The door opened with a loud creak, Mrs. Freely putting her shoulder to it to push it all the way open, and then she waved us inside, rings flashing.

"Come on, come on," she urged. "Lots to do today!"

That didn't really make me want to put a move on, but I followed everyone else inside and then almost immediately gasped.

It wasn't the size of the house or even the massive tree trunk rising up inside the front hallway—although my eyes were trying to take that in—but the *heat*. Outside had been warm, sure. It was Tennessee in June. But inside, it was like a furnace, as though the house were cooking us, and for the first time, Mrs. Freely seemed to falter. "Oh, dear."

We'd all funneled inside, stopping near the front door, and even though there were only ten of us and the room was huge, it was hard to find anywhere to stand where we wouldn't bump into something. There were long tables shoved against the walls, covered in little figures and big glass bells that had flowers underneath them. I counted five fancy, old-fashioned sofas spread across the room, and just as many lamps, all turned off. And this wasn't even an actual *room*, just the front hallway.

Mrs. Freely glanced around, then gestured at Lee to open the windows. "Let some air in here. And where are those fans? We had fans, I thought."

Leigh was looking around, the corners of her mouth turned down, and for one horrifying second, I thought she might start crying.

I was not prepared to deal with adults crying, even if Leigh was only *kind of* an adult.

"There were!" she said. "I set them up this morning like you asked. Before I came to the rec center. I set my alarm for five, and—"

Mrs. Freely held up one hand. "It's all right, honey," she said. "I'm sure you did, and maybe you forgot to lock the door behind you."

"I didn't."

Okay, now Leigh was totally going to cry, and this was officially the worst day and maybe the worst summer ever.

Olivia was standing close to me, and for a moment our eyes met, and I could see that same "ugh, crying" fear on her face. The boys were still looking around the house, but Susanna looked as worried as Olivia did that there might be tears.

But Mrs. Freely saved the day, walking over and patting Leigh's arm. "I'm sure it was an accident, sweetie, don't worry about it. We'll just look around and see if we can find those fans, and as soon as we get 'em all set up, we'll be right as rain."

Lee had moved over to the windows on the other side of the house, and as he went to open one, he leaned closer to the glass. "They're out in the backyard," he said, but there was a note in his voice like he was asking a question.

Mrs. Freely walked over to the window, and the whole group kind of shuffled along behind her, wanting to see, too. And sure enough, out the back window, we could see a pile of box fans sitting on the grass.

"Kids," Mrs. Freely sighed, but Leigh was standing back, shaking her head.

"I swear I locked the door behind me," Leigh said. "I *know* I did."

Straightening, Mrs. Freely shooed us all away from the

window, telling Lee to go out and get the fans. "We'll get this place cooled off again in no time," she said, "and make sure things are locked up this afternoon."

Leigh was still frowning, arms folded tightly over her chest, but at least she didn't look weepy anymore.

The girl who'd sat with Olivia raised her hand, and Mrs. Freely, who'd just taken a deep breath to launch into another spiel about the house, looked irritated. "Yes, Susanna?"

"If someone got in and tossed the fans, how did they lock the door behind them?"

Mrs. Freely blinked. "Well—" she started, but Susanna wasn't done.

"And if they came in some other way, shouldn't we check the house before we start working? What if there are people hidden or something?"

That got everyone's attention, mine included, and I looked up toward the second floor. "Yeah, it might not be safe," I said, and Mrs. Freely went from a little irritated to full-blown irked.

"I will have Lee and Leigh check the rooms while I tell y'all a little bit about the house," she said.

Garrett stepped forward, flicking his hair out of his eyes. "But Lee has to set up the fans."

Mrs. Freely's neck was turning the same color as her shirt, but her smile stayed in place, even if it seemed more like she was baring her teeth at us than smiling. "Lee is going to set up the fans, Leigh will check the rooms real quick—"

"I should probably check the rooms," Lee offered, "and *Leigh* can set up the fans."

"That's sexist," I offered, both because it kind of was and also to see if I could actually make Mrs. Freely's head explode.

It didn't, but I thought it was coming close when she bit out, "Lee, go check the rooms. Leigh, go set up the fans. I will tell you about the house, and if anyone gets snatched, scream, okay?"

We all stood there, blinking at her, until Lee finally said, "So . . . you meant *me* as the Lee who should check—"

"YES, LEE, I MEANT YOU," Mrs. Freely nearly shouted, and I looked down really fast to keep from laughing. Still not an exploding head, but it seemed like Lee had definitely come the closest.

Taking a deep breath, Mrs. Freely closed her eyes, then tilted her head up to the ceiling like she'd find patience or the will not to kill us all there, and then she lowered her gaze back to us. "All right," she said, the word sighing out of her mouth. "Are y'all ready to learn a little bit about Live Oak House?"

CHAPTER 5

OLIVIA

The day already seemed to be something of a loss, as far as I was concerned. It was hot, we were stuck out . . . wherever this was, and Mrs. Freely was clearly losing control of the situation.

But then she clapped again—I was beginning to realize that was a signal she, Lee, and Leigh used when they could feel things were not going well—and gave us her best smile.

"Obviously we don't want to overload y'all on the first day, so today, we're going to take a little tour of Live Oak House, give you the lay of the land and all that. I think you're going to find a lot to enjoy here."

One of the unfamiliar boys, the dark-haired one, raised his hand. "What's with the tree?" he asked before Mrs. Freely even called on him, and I swear her entire face brightened.

"Isn't it something?" she said, walking down a few steps and resting her hand against the weathered trunk. "This is the tree the entire house was built around."

We all craned our necks to look up at where the tree met the roof. A hole had been cut up there, then sort of sealed around the trunk, allowing the top of the tree out of the house.

It all seemed really weird to me, and I didn't know why anyone would want a tree in their house, but then Mrs. Freely said, "When Felix Wrexhall moved to Tennessee from Georgia, he had this tree shipped from his family's estate. He had lost everything back in Georgia except for his wife, Lucy. He brought her with him, and he wanted something to remind him of his old home." She gave the tree another pat. "It's definitely one of the most unique parts of a very special house, Michael."

So that was the dark-haired kid's name, Michael. I wondered if we might get name tags at some point. That might be helpful.

"What kind of tree is it?" Michael asked, and almost as one, the entire group turned to stare at him.

"It's a live oak tree, honey," Mrs. Freely said at last, and Michael rolled his skinny shoulders beneath his hot-pink T-shirt.

From the other side of the group, I heard Ruby make a choking sound that might have been a laugh.

Stepping away from the tree, Mrs. Freely signaled for the rest of us to follow her toward the back of the house.

"Mr. Matthew kept this place in great condition," she went on as we trudged down a hallway behind her. "And everything in it reflects the varied interests of both Mr. Matthew and his father, Felix."

She paused in front of a closed door with an old-fashioned crystal knob. At the top of the door, there was a little window made of stained glass, and light shone through it, making pretty rainbows on the hardwood. "For example, this room contains Mr. Matthew's mother's doll collection."

"Of course there are creepy dolls," Ruby said from the back of the group, and everyone giggled except me.

Mrs. Freely smiled, but it definitely looked forced. "These dolls are not creepy in the slightest, I promise you," she said, then opened the door, revealing . . .

The creepiest dolls I had ever seen.

The room was small, but it had one huge bay window facing the back of the house, and because the ground sloped down so dramatically at that spot, it gave me a weird feeling like we were hovering over thin air. But I couldn't really focus on that when I was surrounded by white porcelain faces on every side.

There were dolls in a glass-fronted cabinet, dolls perched on a burgundy velvet sofa, and, worst of all, one doll that was about the size of an actual kindergartner propped up in the corner, her arms outstretched, her painted red lips stretched in a wide smile.

I instinctively backed up, and bumped into Ruby.

"Sorry," I murmured, going to move away, but she was staring at the dolls, shaking her head.

"We're all gonna die in this house," she said, and Susanna inched closer to both of us.

"I'm not dusting anything in here," she whispered. "Not one single doll."

Mrs. Freely was still talking about how Felix Wrexhall's wife, Lucy, had collected the dolls from all over the world, and then the redheaded guy moved forward, touching the tall doll's hand.

"Dalton!" Mrs. Freely snapped, and he jumped back, frowning at her.

"What? If we're gonna have to dust them and, like, write them down in notebooks, we'll have to touch them, right?" He shrugged and shoved his hands into his pockets. "Might as well get used to it now."

"I bet you're pretty used to touching dolls," Garrett said from the back of the room, and next to me, Ruby snorted.

Dalton glared back at Garrett, as did Michael, but Garrett just smiled back, tossing his hair out of his eyes with a flick of his head.

I noticed Ruby watching him and could've sworn her cheeks were sort of pink.

That was good. Maybe then Ruby would be distracted and not try to talk to me too much. I could still remember the look on her face when I'd caught her and Emma trying to sneak out. The way she'd rolled her eyes when I'd pointed out that climbing out the window and running through the neighborhood after midnight was bound to be a bad idea. A *dangerous* idea.

She turned her head back toward me, black hair swinging against her jaw, and I looked back at Mrs. Freely before she caught me staring. This summer would go a lot better if Ruby and I could pretend we didn't know each other.

"All right, moving on!" Mrs. Freely trilled, ushering us back out into the hall.

We moved to another door, and Mrs. Freely opened it quickly, telling us it was just the hall bathroom. I caught a glimpse of pale green tile and an old-fashioned claw-foot bathtub, plus what looked to be a *lot* of plants, and then the door closed again and we were moving on.

The kitchen was next. It was a huge room, way bigger than

any kitchen I'd ever seen, and it had clearly already been cleaned. It still looked a little dingy in the bright yellow light coming in the windows—there was a big water stain on the ceiling, and the floorboards were discolored. But when I looked closer, I realized that was because there used to be a lot more *stuff* in this kitchen. A big island in the middle of the room, probably, a stove, maybe some kind of old-timey icebox. All that was gone now with only the big zinc sink left, but all in all, it didn't seem so bad.

Past that was a swinging door to another hallway, this one lined with narrow tables that seemed like they were seconds from collapsing, there was so much stuff on them. Then Mrs. Freely moved us back to the front of the house, where she showed us two parlors on either side of the main foyer. One was crammed full of more furniture—sofas, several chairs, a giant wardrobe—but the other had no furniture at all, just a ton of pictures on the wall.

Mrs. Freely stopped there, gesturing around like she was on a game show, telling us what fabulous prizes we could win.

"The Wrexhalls collected a lot of art over the years, but these are the pieces that were most special to Felix and Mr. Matthew." She pointed up at a painting looming on the far wall. In it, a man with hair so blond it was nearly white stood on the front steps of Live Oak House. He was wearing a pale cream suit, one hand in his pocket, the other resting on top of a silver-headed cane. There was a spotted dog sitting at his feet, and it would've been a pretty portrait if the man in it hadn't been glaring out at us like even though he was dead, he *knew* we were in his house.

"This is Felix Wrexhall," Mrs. Freely said, and then she pointed across the room to another portrait. The man in it was blond, too, but he was standing inside Live Oak House, leaning against the massive tree trunk. He wasn't smiling, either, and his eyes seemed sad somehow, but at least he didn't seem to be angry.

"And that's Mr. Matthew," Mrs. Freely went on, "who was one hundred and three years old when he passed this year."

I looked around at all the pictures on the walls. A lot of them were old black-and-white photographs, some of Live Oak House being built. There was also one of a younger Felix Wrexhall with a pretty, dark-haired lady who was wearing an enormous white hat, a baby swaddled in her arms. Then shots of Live Oak House over the years, plus a few paintings of the house and grounds, nothing that really caught my eye.

Mrs. Freely was still talking about all the art in here, how the most valuable pieces had already been taken out, but these were important for sentimental reasons. I reached down to scratch an itch behind my knee.

As I did, I noticed another framed photograph, this one lower down on the wall, right underneath the chair railing.

It was old, too, clearly from the late 1800s, and showed a family dressed all in white. A man, a woman, an older girl, maybe around fifteen or so, and two little girls, both with the same dark hair as their parents, giant bows holding it back from their faces.

Their *identical* faces.

CHAPTER 6

RUBY

I was just thinking that this little art history lesson might actually be worse than the room of Demon Dolls and wondering when we might have lunch when Olivia suddenly blurted out, "Who are they?"

She was standing near the edge of the group—no surprise there—pointing at a small photograph near the window.

Rising up on my tiptoes, I looked over at it, and then immediately saw why that picture had caught her eye. "Ooh, creepy twins!" I said. "That's what this house needs."

Mrs. Freely shot me a look, then moved over to where Olivia was standing, bending her knees to look at the picture Olivia was pointing to. "Huh," she said, leaning in closer. "No idea. It's possible this was a photograph the family picked up somewhere along the way. Or they could be from Felix's wife's family." She straightened up and nodded toward Felix's portrait, then Matthew's. "Probably not Wrexhalls, though. As you can see, that very blond hair was a family trait."

Olivia nodded back, tugging at the end of her braid, her

face red. Why was talking to other people so hard for her? You opened your mouth and words came out. Sometimes they were the wrong ones, but so what?

Mrs. Freely shooed us out of that room and up the stairs. They were wide enough that we could practically all fit side by side, but we still formed a line, and I looked down at the gold and blue paisley carpet lining the steps as Mrs. Freely said, "On the second floor, we'll find the ballroom, two other parlors, three bedrooms, and one more bathroom."

"All of them filled with cursed objects," I added, and Garrett, who was right beside me, laughed. I looked at him from the corner of my eye, feeling pleased with myself. I liked making people laugh, even if it *did* earn me another look from Mrs. Freely.

Then I glanced back at Garrett and he winked at me.

That was . . . a thing that happened.

I turned away quickly, feeling my face go hot. We looked into the ballroom, but there wasn't much to see. It was huge and . . . grand, I guess? Mirrors, a dark wooden floor, some chairs shoved against walls. The parlors seemed a lot like the ones downstairs, too, plenty of furniture and knickknacks, and I wondered how we were supposed to catalog all this stuff. Which reminded me of something.

Mrs. Freely had stopped in front of one of the bedrooms, and I raised my hand.

"Mrs. Freely? You know how we'll be listing all the stuff in the rooms?"

She folded her hands in front of her. "Yes, Ruby."

"Okay, but. Like. *Every* item?" I asked. "Let's say there's a fake plant in one room, and I notice one of the plastic leaves has fallen off. Do I write, 'creepy blue room, one fake plant, one fake plant leaf'?"

"No, Ruby. Just note the whole items in the room. A team of people will be coming at the end of the summer to do a more official itemization, so—"

"So why are we doing this?"

That was from Dalton, the redheaded guy.

Again, Mrs. Freely smiled that smile that was more like baring her teeth. "Because having a sense of what objects are in what rooms will make it easier for the experts to do their jobs." Her grin broadened and actually started looking a little more genuine. "Think about that! It's almost like *you're* all part of their team, too!"

"I did not sign up for that," I said, and the smile fell from Mrs. Freely's face.

"None of you signed up for this," she reminded me. "You were *assigned* to it as a result of your own actions."

That was fair, so I shrugged and looked over toward Olivia Willingham again. Seriously, what could *she* have done to get in here?

Mrs. Freely opened the door behind her then, waving us to follow her in. It was a pretty big bedroom, way bigger than mine at home, with windows looking out the front of the house. I could see the van we'd ridden in parked on the little road down the hill. It was even hotter up here than it had been downstairs, though, so I hoped we wouldn't be hanging out in here much longer. I was starting to sweat in weird places.

The bedroom was painted a pale pink, with yellowed lace curtains in the windows and lots of heavy, dark furniture. There was a smaller door in one of the walls, and I wondered if that led to a closet or something. Maybe one of those fancy old dressing rooms some houses had. Still, it was so small, a grown person would have to duck to get inside, which didn't seem to make much sense. Maybe it was a storage space or something. I edged closer to it until I was nearly leaning against that little door, wanting to be in the back of the group.

Mrs. Freely stood near the dresser, all of us reflected in the mirror behind her, but sort of dim and misshapen, the glass old and wavy. "This was Mrs. Wrexhall's bedroom," Mrs. Freely told us, "Felix's wife, Mr. Matthew's mother. Back then, it wasn't unusual for a husband and wife to have separate bedrooms."

We all sort of fidgeted at that, and I felt an urge to start giggling even though I wasn't really sure why. But Olivia was pink again, and I didn't think it was from the heat.

Clearing her throat, Mrs. Freely went on, "There really isn't much in this room, but I think it's one of the prettiest in the house, so I wanted to be sure you saw it. As you can see, it has a lovely view, and—"

The soft tinkling of a music box started up somewhere nearby, playing some sad-sounding tune, and I nearly stamped my foot.

"Oh, come *on*," I said, and Mrs. Freely stopped talking, looking at me with raised eyebrows.

"Something wrong, Ruby?"

I stared back at her for a second, then waved one hand. "Creepy music boxes? Were the dolls not enough?"

But Mrs. Freely just frowned at me, and then I realized that the other kids in the group were all watching me with weird looks on their faces, too. Susanna was scowling, while Dalton and Michael looked confused. I couldn't see Wesley's face, but even Garrett was watching me with his head tipped slightly to one side.

And it's not like the music was *faint*. I could hear it like someone was holding a music box right next to me.

"Seriously," I said, looking around. "None of you hear that?"

Taking a deep breath, Mrs. Freely put her hands on her hips. "Ruby," she said. "We have a lot of days to get through together in this house, so if you could keep the silliness to a minimum, I'd appreciate that."

I gaped at her. "Okay, one, I never keep silliness to a minimum, but two, I'm not being silly right now! I hear a music box!"

Mrs. Freely just kept staring me down, and the other kids had clearly gotten bored with this whole thing. Dalton and Michael were edging toward the door, and Susanna was still shooting me a dirty look while Garrett was nudging the floorboard with his toe.

I looked over at Wesley, but once again, all I could see was hair.

The music box was still plinking away like something out of a bad horror movie as Mrs. Freely said, "Anyway, let's move on." Then I looked over at Olivia.

She wasn't pink anymore. She was pale, and she was looking at the little door right behind me.

"You hear it, don't you?" I asked her, and she jumped a little, her gaze shooting up to meet mine.

"I don't hear anything," she said, but as she hurried out of the room to follow the others, I knew she was lying.

CHAPTER 7

OLIVIA

I climbed into the van later that afternoon, a juice box in one hand. It was kiwi-strawberry, usually my favorite, but it tasted too sweet, making me feel kind of sick to my stomach, and I fiddled with the yellow plastic straw as I sat by the window, waiting to get out of there and go home.

But Wednesday we'd be back, and we'd be in those rooms alone, not in one big group. The thought made my stomach hurt even more than the sugary juice had.

Ruby Kaye got into the van, her black hair sticking to her cheeks, and she was as sweaty as I was. I really hoped the fans would be working when we came back on Wednesday.

On the way out there, Ruby had sat in the back of the van, but she plopped next to me, her eyes focused on my face.

Talking to Ruby was not high on my list of favorite things, but there was no ignoring that stare. "What?" I finally asked.

"You totally heard the music box," she said, and I shifted in my seat, uneasy.

When we'd been in Mrs. Wrexhall's old bedroom, I had definitely thought I'd heard . . . something. And yes, that something had sounded an awful lot like an old-fashioned music box, and okay, maybe it had seemed weird to me when Ruby pointed it out and no one else had seemed to hear it, but it's not like that meant anything.

My bag was still shoved under the seat, and I reached for it, tugging out the extra juice box I'd grabbed at the rec center. "Want it?" I offered, trying to change the subject. Ruby nodded, taking the juice box and stabbing the straw into the top. She slurped the whole box until it started collapsing in on itself with an obnoxious noise.

Her juice box empty, Ruby lowered it with a sigh and then looked over at me. "Now can we talk about the music box?" she asked, and when she tossed the empty box on the seat next to her, I frowned, picking it up and putting it in the front pocket of my backpack.

"It's no big deal," I told her. "Maybe we were closer to where it was playing than anyone else was, so nobody else heard it."

Ruby pulled a strand of her hair over her lips, thinking about that. "We were close to that little door," she said. "Maybe there was a music box in whatever room that door leads to."

"Probably," I said, turning my face to the window.

"Just, you know, a music box, starting up in a room for no reason."

I ignored her. This had been a long enough day without having to talk to Ruby, and I wasn't sure what she was trying to say about the house, but I knew I didn't want to listen.

She must have picked up on that, because she gave a long sigh. "So what did you do to get Camp Chrysalis duty, anyway?"

"I don't want to talk about it," I replied, resting my heels on the edge of the seat.

Ruby crossed her arms over her chest, and for a second, I thought I'd succeeded in getting her to leave me alone.

"What's Emma doing this summer?" she asked, and I squeezed my knees tighter.

"She went to camp," I said, and tugged at the plastic tips of my shoelaces. "Real camp, not like this."

Ruby made a weird noise, and I looked up at her from underneath my bangs. "Cool, guess she can make all new friends there."

My feet thumped to the floor. "Emma never has trouble making friends."

Ruby looked up at the ceiling, her fingers curled around the edge of the bench. "No, keeping them is Em's problem."

"What happened with you two?" The words were out of my mouth so fast that I didn't have time to really think about them, or how I hadn't wanted to talk about Emma with Ruby.

But Ruby looked over at me, surprised. "She didn't tell you?"

"I didn't ask."

One corner of Ruby's mouth kicked up, and she started fiddling with her hair again. "Let me guess: You were just relieved I was gone."

That was too close to the truth, so I didn't say anything.

Ruby sighed and then, in a whisper, said, "She thought I liked Garrett, too."

I felt a flush start creeping up my neck. "What?" I asked, my eyes shooting toward the rearview mirror, where I could see Garrett slumped in the back of the van.

Ruby swatted at my arm. "Omigosh, don't look," she hissed.

But I couldn't not look. Emma had never mentioned a boy to me. Not once. I mean, sure, we talked about cute boys, but they were all guys in bands or on TV. Not *real* boys. How could Emma like a real boy and not tell me?

Ruby was watching me with this weird expression, her nose wrinkled. "You . . . didn't know that?"

Emma had liked a boy. Emma had had a crush, maybe *still* had a crush, and it was big enough that she'd ditched Ruby over it.

And I hadn't known.

Tipping her head back again, Ruby went on, "Anyway, that was it for me and Em. I thought maybe after my grammy died, she'd come around again, but . . ." She trailed off, and I chewed my lower lip.

"I'm really sorry about your grandmother," I told her, and for a second, Ruby went sort of quiet and still, and I saw something really sad flash across her face.

Then the van pulled up to the rec center, and she shrugged whatever it had been off, unbuckling her seat belt. "Anyway," she said, "guess you and me have more in common than hearing a creepy music box."

"What?" I asked her, gathering up my things.

"Emma," she said.

I was about to remind her that Emma was still my sister even if she wasn't Ruby's friend anymore, but then Ruby added, "She shut us both out, didn't she?"

CHAPTER 8

RUBY

"These gym mats smell like armpits," I announced, and Olivia shot me a look from under her brows. We were sitting on the same edge of the mat with our Responsibility Journals, waiting until it was time to go home. This was the other part of our Camp Chrysalis Experience—working at Live Oak House in the morning, writing in these dumb things about how we could be better people in the afternoon. Olivia was scribbling away in hers while all I'd written was, well, *These gym mats smell like armpits.*

"They do," I told her, trying to find a comfy way to sit. Susanna was on the other side of the mat, and she looked over her shoulder, nodding at me.

"Totally armpits," she agreed, wrinkling her nose. "It's gross."

"This whole place is gross," I said. "Rec center? More like *get rekt* center."

Susanna snorted at that, which was a nice change from Olivia's dirty looks. I reminded myself not to get carried away and keep making jokes, something I always had trouble with, but I still added, "That's what I should put in my Responsibility Journal—'I am *not* responsible for the smell of the rec center.'"

"'I'm not responsible for throwing up if they keep giving us that nasty juice,'" Susanna added, scooting closer, and I grinned at her.

"'I'm not responsible for how Lee does his hair.'"

We both looked across the gym at Lee, who was sitting on one of the bleachers, his spiky blond hair sticking up over his forehead, and Susanna laughed.

"Who *is* responsible for how he does his hair?" she asked. "Because we should talk to that person. *That* person should be at Camp Chrysalis."

I scribbled that down in my journal, and Olivia looked up from her notebook, a crease between her brows. "You know Mrs. Freely is gonna read these, right? You'll get in trouble."

I hadn't known that, but I sat up anyway, spreading my arms wide. "What kind of trouble?" I asked. "Sent to a dorky camp, made to count the creepy things inside it? That's already happened, so I really don't know how this could get much worse."

Olivia opened her mouth to answer, but I cut her off before she could. "I am making my own fun," I told her, "and maybe if you did the same thing, you'd have a better summer."

"We're not here to have fun," Olivia argued, her voice sharper than I'd heard from her before—Olivia Willingham was definitely not a fan of mine, but she'd never really snapped at me or anything. I always thought of her as Quieter Emma, to be honest. But now her cheeks were red and her eyes were bright, and even though she was mad, I thought this was probably the more interesting Olivia.

I kind of wanted to see what Mad Olivia Willingham was like.

"They don't want us to have fun," I shot back, aware that some of the other kids were looking over now. "That doesn't mean we can't have it. Loosen up."

For a second, I thought Olivia might respond. She looked like she really wanted to, her free hand clenching at her side, but in the end, she just shook her head and went back to her journal. "This is stupid," she muttered, "and we're supposed to be writing, not arguing."

"We were arguing over what we were writing," I reminded her, but she didn't even look up.

I realized then that one of the other boys I hadn't recognized—Dalton, I knew now—had moved closer to our mat, probably to see what was going on with us. He wasn't as tall as Garrett, and his hair wasn't red so much as orange. There was a smattering of freckles across his cheeks and nose, and his T-shirt looked about three sizes too big. The hot pink seriously clashed with his hair. I was about to tell him that and suggest he make a complaint when he dodged forward and snatched Olivia's journal out of her hands.

"Hey!" she cried, scrambling to her feet, but Dalton was already moving away, grinning wide. His front teeth were crooked, and there was something green caught between them, which was gross since I *knew* we had not had anything green to eat today.

"'I need to be more responsible for myself,'" Dalton read out in a high-pitched voice. "'I need to realize that not everyone cares about the same things that I do, and that I am not responsible for Emma.'"

I looked over at Olivia, waiting for her to launch herself at Dalton and tear the journal out of his hands, but she was just . . . standing there. Like she'd been frozen. Her face had been pink before, but it was white now, and she was blinking like she might cry. But her hands were clutched into fists again, so why didn't she *use* them? We were already Bad Kids, after all. Might as well throw down.

Dalton was also expecting her to come after him, I think, because he looked over at her and his smile suddenly faltered. In that second, I pushed forward and snatched the journal out of his hands.

"Don't be a jerk," I told him, tilting my head to look up at him. Everyone was taller than me these days. It was deeply annoying.

"You're the one who was fighting with her," he fired back, but I could tell he didn't really mean it. His voice cracked on the last word, and I glared up at him even harder.

"We weren't fighting, we were *talking*, and I've known her forever. You haven't, so you don't get to pick on her. Now go back over there with the other dude from *Greene County*"—I let scorn drip from my voice even though for all I knew, Greene County was made of mansions and gold streets—"and leave us alone."

Dalton still had a little fight left in him, I guess, because he looked down at me, his blue eyes narrowing slightly. "And if I don't?"

"I'll take a picture of you in that shirt and put it on the internet," I said, and apparently that was the right threat, because he made a snorting sound with a "Whatever," but ambled back to his spot on the other mats. Olivia had picked up her journal from where I'd tossed it and was dusting off the cover even though, from what I could see, it was fine.

"Boys," I said to her with a shrug, and she nodded, still not looking at me.

"Thanks," she mumbled, and I waved it away.

"No big. I mean, I don't like you or anything, but I like bullies even less, so . . ."

I let that trail off, watching Olivia. She lifted her head and looked at me, tilting her head a little like she was trying to figure out what to think.

Honestly, I didn't know what to think myself. Defending Olivia Willingham was a weird thing for me, but like I said, I hate bullies, and Olivia may be kind of stuck-up and a major stickler for rules, but she's not *mean*.

In the end, she sat down with her journal again, turning her back to me and Susanna. I sat down, too, and spent the rest of the time actually writing in my journal, and not stupid stuff, either. I actually wrote, *I need to be responsible with my words,* and weirdly enough, I think I meant it.

CHAPTER 9

OLIVIA

Walking into my house, I was hit by air-conditioning, so cold I nearly shivered. Still, it felt good after being hot for so much of the day, and I followed Mom down the hallway, toward the kitchen. We'd talked a little bit about my day on the ride home, but I hadn't wanted to get into a lot of what had happened, either at the house or the rec center later, and I was glad she wasn't asking any more questions. I just wanted to get something to drink, maybe grab a snack, and go huddle up in my room for a while.

But as soon as I got into the kitchen, my phone started making the blooping sound that meant someone was trying to get me on Hangouts.

And the only person that could be was Em.

Pulling my phone out of my pocket, I leaned against the island in the middle of the kitchen, crossing one ankle behind the other and answering my sister's call.

Her face filled the screen. *My* face.

"Oh, gosh, you're home!" she said, smiling at me, and I made myself smile back.

She was sitting somewhere, probably in her cabin since I could make out a bunk bed behind her, and she had the phone close to her face.

"Yup, we're done at three every day," I told her, and out of the corner, I saw Mom duck her head in real quick. I thought she might call out to Emma, but maybe she wanted us to have some alone time, because she flashed me a quick smile and disappeared again.

"Was it fun?"

I looked at Emma and tried to figure out if she was making fun of me or if she felt guilty or what. It was the weirdest thing, not being able to work out how she felt. I used to think that because we were twins, not only did we share a face, but we must share a brain too. There had been times when I could look at Em and know exactly what she was thinking. But she'd gone from being the other half of me to some new, whole person who felt like a secret.

Who liked boys and didn't tell me about it.

"Not really, but it wasn't bad," I lied, holding my phone with one hand and opening the fridge with the other. I pulled out a pitcher of sweet tea. "Ruby Kaye is there."

Em wrinkled her nose. "I haven't talked to her in forever."

"Yeah, she told me that," I said, pouring myself a glass of tea, and on the screen, Emma frowned.

"You talked to her?" she said. "I thought you didn't like her."

"I don't," I said quickly, and it was true, I didn't. Even if she had been nice about the journal thing. Well, not *nice* really, but . . . protective.

Which was weird.

"She told me you guys fought over a boy," I said, trying to sound casual, like finding out about this Garrett guy hadn't been a shock.

Emma shook her head. "It wasn't about a boy, it was just . . . you know, Ruby being Ruby." She shrugged. "I got tired of her. Always being so—"

"Ruby," I finished for her, and she nodded.

"Exactly."

I didn't point out that as far as I could tell, Ruby Kaye was the same as she'd always been, and that Emma had liked her a lot before that. And I didn't tell her what Ruby said, about Emma suddenly shutting both of us out. Because it wasn't true, not really. So Emma was trying new things, and had done one really stupid thing. She had learned her lesson, probably, and, I reminded myself again, it's not like she had asked me to take the fall for her.

So why did I still feel so awful about it?

I carried the phone back toward my room. "Anyway, it was an okay day, I guess," I told her. "Not my favorite way to spend the summer, but it's not like I had anything else going on."

On the screen, Emma leaned in closer, dropping her voice. "Are you by yourself?" she asked, and I walked into my room and closed the door behind me with my foot.

"Now I am."

Emma tucked a strand of hair behind her ear, the phone wobbling in her hand. "I really feel bad. I'm going to make this up to you, Livvy, I promise."

We had never argued about what had happened that day. I hadn't known how to feel about any of it, Emma taking the lipstick, me saying I'd done it, Emma letting me take the blame. It all felt confusing, a million different feelings tangled up into one big knot of ugliness that I hadn't wanted to unravel.

And I still didn't really want to. "It's okay," I told her, even though we both knew it wasn't.

"It was so stupid," Emma went on, "and I don't even know why I did it. I guess I just wanted to see if I could?" She shook her head. "But, I mean, hey, you're getting to do something this summer after all, I guess!"

It wasn't all that different from what I'd been thinking, but I still didn't like hearing Emma say it. "Yeah," I finally said. "And the house is kind of neat."

When there wasn't a spooky music box playing that only me and Ruby could hear, I added in my head, and Emma beamed at me. "Awesome!" she said, and I could hear more than enthusiasm in her voice. She was *relieved.* If I made it seem like Camp Chrysalis was fun, she wouldn't have to feel so guilty.

Did I *want* her to feel guilty?

I didn't know. So I just said, "Anyway, I really need to take a shower now. It was so hot today."

Em nodded. "Gotcha. I'm about to have to leave for canoeing anyway."

"Super," I said weakly, and if Emma noticed anything weird in my expression, she ignored it.

"Talk to you tomorrow, okay, Livvy?"

"Yeah. Have fun."

She waggled her fingers at me, then the screen went blank, and I stood there, holding my phone in one hand and my tea in the other before tossing the phone onto my bed.

When Em and I had gotten our own bedrooms last year, I'd wanted a big bed. We'd always had bunk beds or two twin beds in our old room, so getting something big felt like a way of making my new room feel different. Like mine. Mom found this pretty queen-sized bed with tall white bedposts and a headboard that rose up in a curving arc. For a week or so, it had been against the wall across from my window, but then I'd asked Dad to help me move it against a corner, making a space between the headboard and the walls.

That's where I headed then, kicking off my shoes, climbing onto the bed, and clambering over the headboard to drop into that little nook formed between the bed and the corner.

I'd made it a pretty comfy space with extra pillows, some blankets, and a stack of books, plus the stuffed animals that I was too embarrassed to have out in my room but wasn't quite ready to get rid of yet.

Mom called it my "cave," Dad said it was like "a tree house minus the tree," and Emma had said it was "weird."

That hadn't stopped her from wanting to sit back there with me, though, and we'd spent lots of afternoons crammed in, eating cookies and talking. But I was glad not to have to share that day, and I snuggled down onto the pillows, pulling out a paperback, the cover wrinkled from the time I accidentally set it down next to the pool and it got wet.

I sat back there for a long time, reading and feeling myself unknot. Between the creepiness at the house and then everything with my journal back at the rec center, I felt like I'd been twisted into a pretzel. But thinking about Dalton and my journal reminded me of how Ruby Kaye had gotten my journal back for me.

Laying the book on my chest, I looked up at the ceiling and thought about that. Had Ruby meant it when she said she was the only one who got to pick on me? Maybe it was a town loyalty thing. In any case, it had been . . . nice. Surprising, definitely.

Then I thought about the ballroom again, the shadow in the mirror, and frowned.

I could really do without any more surprises this summer.

CHAPTER 10

RUBY

"There are working bathrooms here, right?"

We were all standing in the front hall of Live Oak House that Wednesday morning, notebooks at the ready, Mrs. Freely wearing another Camp Chrysalis T-shirt, this one in bright blue. Still had that creepy smiling head on it, though, and her own smile as she looked over at me seemed a little forced.

"Pardon?" she asked, and I glanced around at my fellow campers. Olivia was hanging near the back of the group, pulling at the hem of her T-shirt, and all the boys were sort of grouped together except for Wesley, who hovered near my elbow. Susanna had her arms folded over her chest, one hip thrust out, clearly over it already.

This was our first morning of actual work, and we all had the little pink notebooks we'd been given for listing the stuff in the house. I had already written in mine, big letters across the top page that said, *Stuff in a room that's not one of the creepy ones.* I was hoping that might act as a sort of charm to ensure I didn't end up in the doll room, or that bedroom with the music box playing.

Mrs. Freely pointed to the hallway over to the left of the stairs. "There's plumbing in the house, but this is the only bathroom that's functional right now. If you need to use it, make sure you find me, Lee, or Leigh and let us know."

"So we have to make an announcement if we need to pee?" I asked. "Because that could be embarrassing for some people. I obviously don't have a problem with it, but I want to make sure my fellow campers—"

"You can come tell me privately if you need to," Mrs. Freely cut in, and I frowned. Truth be told, I was wondering how long I could put off the part where we'd be sent out into the house to start cataloging things. Sometimes that worked in class, getting a teacher off the subject, pretending to be really interested in stories from her childhood or whatever, and oops, next thing you know, we'd run out of time to do all those math problems. I was really good at that in school, but apparently Mrs. Freely wasn't so easily distracted.

Or maybe I just hadn't found the right thing yet.

Mrs. Freely went on, "Susanna, Michael, and Dalton, you'll take this front room down here. Olivia and Ruby, the servants' passage upstairs has your name on it."

Olivia and I glanced at each other, and she tugged at the end of her braid.

My hand shot up.

"Mrs. Freely?" I asked. "Olivia and I don't actually work well together."

Pressing her lips together, Mrs. Freely lowered the clipboard a bit. "Well, that's the point of all this, Ruby, to *learn* to work well together. Now, Garrett, you—"

"But what if we fight?" I continued. "Like, a real brawl with hair pulling and scratching and someone puts it on YouTube, and then everyone is like, 'Oh, yeah, Camp Chrysalis, that's where those two girls fell out a window during a fight and became a viral sensation.'"

There was total silence following that, and for a moment, Mrs. Freely blinked at me while the other kids stared with wide eyes.

Finally, Mrs. Freely muttered something to herself that sounded like, "First week, it's the first week."

"Fine," she said, louder and with that fixed smile back in place. "Garrett, *you* help Ruby in the hallway, and Olivia, you can take the ballroom upstairs. Would that work for everyone?"

I gave Mrs. Freely a thumbs-up. "You know it, girl."

I waited for Mrs. Freely to say something about that, hoping it might be the distraction I was looking for, but she just went back to her clipboard. "And that leaves Wesley down here with me."

Wesley didn't seem all that happy, but he didn't say anything because clearly he was a wuss.

"Now then!" Mrs. Freely said brightly. "Everyone ready?"

"As we'll ever be!" I called back.

I followed Garrett toward the stairs. The day was already hot, and there was sweat behind my knees, which was a deeply icky feeling.

But I remembered the hallway from our little tour on Monday. There were a lot of tables with little knickknacks and some paintings, but it didn't seem so bad.

Garrett didn't seem so bad, either. He was about a head taller than me, and his hair was super blond, flopping over his forehead. He had freckles across his nose, and I liked the way his eyes were green and brown at the same time. I didn't know Garrett all that well, since he was a year older than me, but I saw him around school, plus his family went to Grammy's church. I'd seen him there on the Sundays I'd gone with her. That was one of our favorite things to do, actually. I'd spend the night on a Saturday, then Sunday, she'd take me to her church, and afterward, we'd go to the Chesterfield Inn for their lunch buffet.

"So what are you in for?" I joked as we made our way up the stairs.

He only smirked and shook his head, so I shrugged, tapping my pen on the front cover of my "logbook."

"If you don't tell me, I'm going to go ahead and assume murder," I said, which made him chuckle, but he still didn't give me an answer.

We stopped on the landing, facing a short hallway, and at the end of it, there was a door. It was made out of the same light wood as the floor, and there was a pretty stained glass window in the center. If there had been enough light back here, I bet it would have made colors on the walls and floor, but it was kind of dim, so the stained glass—which had to be expensive—seemed like a waste.

Garrett pressed on the door handle, and it opened, revealing a narrow hallway.

I frowned. "Why put a door in the middle of a hallway that leads to another hallway?"

It was Garrett's turn to shrug. "Rich people," he muttered, like that explained it all.

And hey, maybe it did. Maybe separating hallways with fancy doors was a fun thing to do if you were rich.

Or maybe this was a different kind of hallway. Mrs. Freely had called it "the servants' passage." And after all, the one we'd just walked through had been empty and, like, normal hall-ish. This one?

It was so crammed full of stuff that Garrett and I had to walk down it single file rather than side by side.

There were those same long tables and glass bells I'd seen in the front of the house. I crouched down to look at the nearest one, peering through the dusty glass at a taxidermy chipmunk perched on a fake branch.

"Great," I muttered. "We got the Dead Animal Hall, I guess."

Garrett snorted, putting his bucket down. According to our instructions from Mrs. Freely, we needed to make a list of everything on the tables. That hadn't sounded that hard, really, but looking at all of it now, I wanted to sweep everything to the floor and say there hadn't actually been any stuff back here.

Maybe Garrett felt the same way, because he stared at the tables for a second, putting his hands in his back pockets and sighing.

It was dim back here, and a good deal cooler than the rest of the house, with a tiny window set high up on the far wall that let in some light. The top half of the hallway was covered in dark green wallpaper with big, blooming pink roses all over it. The paper was only starting to peel up at the edges, but there was a thick layer of dust on the floor, and it was clear that no one had been back here in a long time.

"This is stupid," Garrett murmured on a sigh, and I had to agree with him. Who cared about this stuff, anyway? It all looked like junk to me.

"You know, they call this the Hall of Heads," Garrett said as he lifted a dusty glass bell off a stuffed bird and studied it.

Seeing as how he'd only said like five words so far today, that was a weird conversation starter. I echoed Garrett's last words. "The Hall of Heads?"

"Uh-huh," he said, tapping the taxidermy bird. It wobbled on its branch, looking like it might explode into a mass of dust and feathers if you breathed on it wrong, but I didn't say anything. I wasn't Garrett's mom or Mrs. Freely, and if he wanted to make a mess, that was on him. "My brother and some of his friends tried to spend the night here right after the old man died," he went on, "and ended up talking to this old guy the city hired to cut the grass. He said people who've worked here say they see a head floating toward them down this hall, over and over. It starts at one end, zooms down"—he lifted his arm, fingers still covered in dust, making a sort of zooming motion, complete with a *vrooooom!* sound effect—"then starts all over again."

I crossed my arms, looking at the far end of the hallway, past the tables with all their junk. In this particular spot, the hall was long enough and the one window was so shaded by the heavy trees outside that you couldn't even see the far end all that well. It was kind of easy to imagine a head zooming out of that gloom, and while I didn't spook that easy, I also didn't like picturing it. I looked back over at Garrett with a frown.

"You should try not talking," I told him. "Not talking might be a really good look on you."

He shrugged in reply and pulled the logbook out of his back pocket. "Just thought you might want to know what we're dealing with here," he said as he jotted something down.

"Whose head?" I asked, taking out my own book and moving to the table on the other side of the hall. This one held a few clocks as well as a stack of books so old, I couldn't even read the titles on their spines.

"Huh?" Garrett lifted his head, his blond hair falling over his eyes. He flicked it back with a quick jerk that was probably really appealing to some girls, but definitely didn't make *my* stomach flutter or anything.

I want that officially on the record, by the way. I do not have a crush on Garrett McNamara.

Anyway.

"The head," I said, and pointed back at the far end of the hall. "The *vroom-vroom* head. It has to belong to someone, right? Can't have independent heads whooshing around. So whose head is it?"

Garrett looked at me with a V between his eyebrows, like he was trying to figure out if I was being serious or not. I stared at him, fists on my hips. "Dude," I said. "I'm always serious when it comes to floating severed heads."

He grinned at that, a sudden smile that lit up his face, and ugh, that was so annoying. I did not want to deal with a cute boy this summer.

Okay, anyway, he grinned in a totally normal way that didn't do anything to his face at all except show his teeth, which are normal, okay-looking teeth. And then he said, "I don't know. How many ghosts are supposed to be in this place, anyway?"

That was the first I'd heard of any ghosts, to be honest. Look, I'm not stupid, I could tell a place like Live Oak House would be haunted as heck. I've seen TV and watched movies. But I'd never really paid any attention to it or any of the stories about it since spooky stuff has never been my thing. And that music box thing had to just be a trick of . . . acoustics or something. Old houses were weird like that.

"No idea," I said. "What are the stories?"

"I think someone died the first day they started building the house," he replied. "Or that's what my brother said. And something really bad happened to make that Wrexhall guy move here. Like, a fire, I think? He definitely didn't have any family except for his wife, and she was really weird. Collecting the dolls, not wanting to go into town. Eventually they sent her off to some hospital in Nashville and she never came back. But there's probably more," he went on, moving down the table. I could see now that he was writing in his logbook *Dead thing* and *Other dead thing.* "There were stories about this place since forever, even before the old guy who lived here died. It only got *worse* after he was gone. Like, when my older brother and his friends dared each other to spend the night alone in here, it was . . . it was bad."

That was interesting. "What happened?" I asked.

Garrett gave another one of those shrug/hair flick things. "The cops showed up, nearly arrested them for trespassing."

"Oh," I replied. That was hardly the spine-chilling tale of terror I'd been expecting, although I guess that had been scary in its own way.

We went back to listing things quietly for a while, and this is going to sound crazy, but as I made my lists and started making my way down the hall, I had pretty much forgotten about the head. I know, how does someone *forget* that there's a story about a flying severed head coming from the very direction you're headed toward?

Like I said, I was never all that interested in the spooky. As I wrote, I was mostly thinking about when I'd get to leave, how to turn this whole stupid day into a story for my friends on Xbox later. They'd like it, I thought, especially if I added the part about the Hall of Heads, and also maybe made it seem like the thing I'd done to end up in the situation was a lot cooler than anything involving glitter. Ooh, and maybe I could even build my own Hall of Heads in Minecraft! Turning this whole thing into a video game universe might actually be cool.

Maybe then this whole summer wouldn't feel like such a waste.

CHAPTER 11

OLIVIA

I never minded cleaning my room when Mom asked me to. Taking care of my own space and all that. I'd even painted the walls pink, something Em never would've gone for. Anyway, the point is, it's not the cleaning that I minded when Mrs. Freely sent me off with a pack of glass wipes and my little itemization notebook, pointing up the stairs and telling me I could "start in the ballroom."

It was that I'd be doing it alone.

I got it. The house was big, she needed us to divide and conquer.

But if you'd ever been in Live Oak House, you'd understand why the idea of being all by myself in the ballroom upstairs had me feeling cold even on a hot day.

There were twenty-three rooms there. That's what Mrs. Freely had said, and it seemed like a lot. What kind of rooms were they?

That was the thought that kept going through my head as I walked up the stairs to the ballroom. What if there were more rooms than anyone thought? Were there spaces hidden behind the walls? Secret doors you could open with the press of a hidden switch? I know the idea of those things would've thrilled Emma, but to me, it was just creepy. I've always liked knowing exactly where everything is.

Being able to expect things makes life a lot less stressful, I think.

The ballroom was off to the left of the grand staircase, and while I thought it was weird to put a ballroom upstairs, when I stopped on the landing and looked behind me, I suddenly understood why it had been built that way. The staircase swept down, widening as it got to the bottom, and I imagined how fancy dresses would've looked, the skirts brushing over the dark blue carpet lining the wooden stairs.

Then I remembered there had never been any balls in this house. No parties, no groups of people, no fancy dresses at all. Felix Wrexhall built this room because that's what big houses were supposed to have back then, a ballroom. The only people who'd ever been in this one were him, his wife, and their son.

Weirdly enough, that made me kind of sad. This whole house was sad, really, like a birthday present that someone never got to open. All this pretty wrapping, all for nothing.

Thinking that didn't make me feel any better as I held my plastic bucket in one hand and used the other to push open one of the big doors that led to the ballroom.

It was brighter inside than I'd imagined it would be, which definitely made me feel a little bit better. The windows faced the front of the house, and a big set of French doors led out onto a balcony. Overhead, there was what I guessed was a chandelier, but it was covered in a black plastic trash bag, dust making the bag almost look gray.

Ew.

Pushing my shoulders back, I walked farther into the room.

Downstairs, I could hear Mrs. Freely cheerfully ordering kids to different parts of the house, and I tried to tell myself I was lucky to get the ballroom. It was big, sure, but it only took a few minutes to note everything that was in the room—thirteen chairs covered with cloths, and the chandelier—and then all I had to do was clean the mirrors.

No big.

Sure, there were a lot of them. They lined the back wall, and I looked really small in them, a dozen Olivias in too-bright T-shirts. What would it have been like to come into this room as a guest, in one of those fancy ball gowns? For a second, I stood there looking at myself, and then I pulled out one side of my T-shirt with one hand, giving a wobbly curtsy. I laughed because I looked so stupid, but the sound seemed to echo in the big room. It felt dumb to be creeped out when I knew there were darker, spookier places in the house I could be instead—the idea of setting foot in that doll room made me shudder—but I was suddenly really mad at myself for saying I didn't want to be on a team. Even if I wasn't crazy about some of these other kids, it would've been better than being up here on my own.

"Bad call, Past Olivia," I muttered to myself, then moved toward the mirrors, the package of glass wipes in my hand.

I frowned at the bright yellow daisy on the label. This was

the organic stuff with no harsh chemicals, what my mom called "crunchy granola stuff." I guess no one wanted kids breathing toxic fumes. That made sense. Unfortunately, the stuff didn't work all that great.

I started to clean. Well, it felt less like cleaning and more like smearing smudges around, but it was the best I could do. I couldn't even reach the top of the glass, and I wondered if I should go ask for a ladder or something. But if Mrs. Freely didn't want us having real glass cleaner, there was no way she was letting us climb ladders.

And as I stared at the top of those mirrors lining the ballroom, clearly out of reach, I realized something really important: We weren't actually here to get this place up to snuff or whatever it was Mrs. Freely had said. We *couldn't*. It would take a team of professional cleaners to do that. We were just here to fill our days. To be punished because we'd been bad.

Except I *hadn't* done anything bad, Em had, and suddenly it hit me how stupid and unfair this all was. This whole time, I'd been trying to tell myself that hey, at least I was spending my summer doing something productive. But no, this was a way to keep us out of trouble.

It was pointless.

I stood there staring at the mirror, and that feeling I'd had the first morning at the rec center came back again. The crying feeling.

I hadn't given in to it then, and I wasn't going to now. Not on the first day like some baby who was upset she'd gotten in trouble.

I sniffed hard and swabbed at the mirror. Okay. Okay, maybe this was supposed to be a punishment and a waste of my time, but that didn't mean I had to treat it like one. I could still make this whole thing whatever I wanted it to be, could *still* point at Live Oak House and say, "I helped make that place pretty." Power of positive thinking.

I cleaned as much of the mirror as I could, even getting down on my hands and knees to clean near the bottom. The baseboards down there were dusty and gross, so I cleaned those, too, even though I'm not sure the glass wipes were all that effective.

I was thinking about going to ask Mrs. Freely if she had something else when I heard music drifting out from the hallway.

And not just any music.

The same music I'd heard that first day, the music box sounds coming from behind that one door.

Frowning, I got up and approached the doors to the ballroom, then stuck my head out, looking up and down the hall. The bedroom we'd been in when I'd heard the music the other day was nearby, and sure enough, that seemed to be where the music was coming from.

I stood there for a second, trying to decide what to do. I could ignore it and get back to cleaning. That seemed like the best option. Safe, sensible, all of that.

Or I could go to the bedroom and see for myself where that music was coming from.

Hesitating, I waited for . . . I don't know, some kind of sign? Maybe for the music to stop so I wouldn't have to choose.

But it kept playing, and then suddenly my feet were moving toward that bedroom and its little door.

CHAPTER 12

RUBY

"How is this supposed to take us all day?"

I looked up from the table of knickknacks to see Garrett staring down the hall, his own notebook in hand.

"I mean," he went on, "it's not like there's that much back here. It's . . . like, 'here's a bird,' 'here's a book.'"

Lifting his head, Garrett shrugged at me. "Should we go ask them for something else to do?"

I was sitting on the floor with my notebook resting on my knees. So far, I'd only cataloged five things, but I'd really spent my time on those five entries, drawing elaborate pictures of them, using fancy, curlicue script. I reminded myself that next time, I should totally bring colored pencils or something, really draw this whole thing out.

Heh. *Draw* it out.

But now I stared at Garrett. "Dude," I said, shaking the notebook at him. "The more time we take on one little thing, the less we have to do. Get your head in the game."

He grinned at that, that stupid grin that made my cheeks go

hot, and I looked back at my notebook, studiously making little scallop designs around the words *Really old book (older than other old book on line 2)*. "Good point," he said. "And I guess that means I could also do this."

Taking his pencil, he pressed it down hard on the cover of his notebook until the point snapped, the sound loud in the quiet hallway.

"Oh no," he said in a flat voice. "I seem to have broken my pencil."

I gave him my best solemn face. "Guess you'll have to go get a new one," I said. "And maybe even sharpen it. Could really take some time."

"Thirty minutes at least," he said, and I screwed up my face at him.

"An hour if you were really serious about it."

He grinned again, flipping his hair out of his eyes, and ugh, ugh, ugh.

But then he nodded back at the door. "You'll be okay back here by yourself?"

I wasn't sure if I should be insulted by that or not, but it did kind of feel like a reminder that Garrett *was* a year older than me, and while I might be sitting here thinking he was cute, he could just as easily be standing *there* thinking that I was a little kid.

I didn't like that feeling.

In the end, I gave him a thumbs-up and he headed out, the door to the hallway swinging closed behind him.

Sighing, I looked back at my notebook, then lifted my gaze to the tables of stuff. There was still one more under the window that I could get to, but I didn't really see the point. Like I'd told Garrett, the longer we could draw this out, the better, as far as I was concerned, so I flipped to an empty page and started doodling.

First I did a cartoon version of the bird under the bell jar, but I made it bigger than it really was, giving it fangs and wings that ended in sharp tips. For added weirdness, I gave it heavy eyebrows, smiling as my giant creepy bird took shape on the page.

"Total Fridge Material," I muttered to myself, almost without thinking, but then my pencil stuttered on the page.

That's what Grammy had said about my drawings. Whenever I went to her house after school, she'd ask what I'd drawn that day, and if it was weird enough, she'd pronounce it "Total Fridge Material."

All those drawings were in the boxes now, the ones still in our garage from when Mom had cleaned out Grammy's place. We only had a few things left to go through, but we'd been putting it off. We weren't saying why, but I knew that for me, it felt like the last little link to Grammy. Once we were done with that, what else would there be?

Clearing my throat and scrubbing at the sudden stinging in my eyes, I flipped to another blank page, and this time I didn't draw any of my own stuff, only monsters from video games I liked.

I'd just finished a pretty good Creeper (if I do say so myself) when I heard the hallway door open.

"Duuuuuude," I drawled out. "You were only gone for like five minutes! Weak!"

Grinning, I lifted my head.

But while the hallway door was open, there was no sign of Garrett.

That was . . . not cool.

Especially because I remembered how the door had slammed behind me and Garrett when we'd first come in, and how it had slammed again behind Garrett when he left. There was something about the hinges that made it close on its own, maybe for fire code reasons or something, maybe because the house was old, and for all I knew, there was a slant or something to the floor.

But the point was, that door had closed on its own, and now it was open.

Halfway.

Which would be impossible.

"Garrett?" I called, because I really, really wanted to believe this was still some kind of prank. Maybe he'd wedged it a certain way and had ducked back into the hall, laughing at me.

If that was the case, all the smiles and hair flicks in the world would not save him. I would stab him with his newly sharpened pencil and possibly kick him somewhere painful.

"This isn't funny!" I called, then immediately rolled my eyes at myself. Great, just a few spooky seconds and I was already talking like someone in a bad horror movie.

"Seriously! If you're being a jerk, I'm going to make you list all the dead stuff by yourself!"

Still nothing, but the door didn't move.

I slowly got to my feet, my back still against the wall, the notebook slipping from my fingers to land on the hardwood floor. Okay. Okay, I would walk over to the door and see if Garrett was out there myself.

No big. I had this.

"You are brave," I said out loud to myself, feeling comforted and stupid all at the same time. "You are a warrior woman who can play Silent Hill with the lights out. You can walk over to a door."

I inched down the hallway. "See, look? You're doing it now! You are walking toward that door." I kept my voice pitched low, just in case Garrett was waiting there to jump out at me or laugh, but I couldn't seem to stop talking, the flow of words making it easier to keep moving. "So brave, so not scared of creepy houses or open doors. Who's scared of a door? Not this girl, that's who. And Garrett, if you're out there and listening to me, you should be scared, because I will murderize you super hard for this."

There was no reply, and in my heart, I knew Garrett wasn't out there, but there was something weird about the silence. It felt . . . weighted. Heavy, somehow, like someone was waiting on the other side of that door, holding their breath.

I seemed to be holding mine, too, my chest tight as I eased myself right up to the door.

It still stood there, half open, and there was a part of me almost expecting it to shut in my face, and a sudden, awful image rose up in my mind of taking hold of the door, only to have it slam and catch my fingers or something.

I shuddered at that and was about to take a step back when I heard something from out in the hallway.

Music.

Not just any music, but the same sad, soft music box melody I'd heard on that first day. The music playing behind the little door in the second-floor bedroom, the music everyone claimed not to hear except for me.

And Olivia. Even though she'd said she hadn't.

It was hard to make myself ease out of the doorway and into the hall, my brain still shouting that the door was going to close and squash me, but I did it, letting out a long breath once I was safely in the hallway.

I turned back around to look at the door, and from the bigger hallway, that small, cramped hall with its tables of junk seemed . . . spookier somehow. Darker.

And then, as I watched, the door very slowly swung closed.

Swallowing hard, I backed up, nearly tripping over my untied shoelaces.

"Old houses are weird," I muttered to myself again. "So weird, doing weird things because . . . architecture."

But I could still hear the music box playing, and even though my stomach was queasy and my knees felt kind of weak, I made myself turn down the hall and walk toward it.

The bedroom was around a corner on the second floor, and I turned it, pushing my shoulders back, determined to find out where that music was coming from.

But someone had already beat me there.

CHAPTER 13

OLIVIA

"**O**hhhhh, you are such a liar!"

I jumped back from the door to see Ruby Kaye standing in the hall, and I scowled.

"I don't know what you're talking about," I said, holding my chin up, and she snorted at me, crossing her arms over her chest and thrusting out a hip. As she did, I glanced down at her shoes. She was wearing turquoise laces in one, red in the other. Who did that, seriously?

"Um, yeah, you do. You heard it, too."

The faint music was still echoing in my ears, and I glanced at the closed bedroom door even as I said, "I didn't hear anything."

Ruby threw her hands up, looking toward the ceiling, "Whyyyyyy?" she groaned before lowering her head to look at me again. That blue streak had come loose from her ponytail, and it swung in front of her eyes. "Why are you being this way?"

She walked toward me, and I found myself taking a step back, even though that was stupid. It wasn't like Ruby was going to fight me or anything. But she wasn't heading for me, she was heading for the door.

Curling her fingers around the antique doorknob, she gave it a rattle, but the door didn't budge.

And then, faintly, the sound of the music box started up again.

Ruby's gaze shot to me, and this time I couldn't even pretend I didn't hear it.

I walked closer to the door, the floorboards squeaking under my sneakers, and leaned in close, facing Ruby.

"Suuuuuch a liar," she whispered, and I held one finger over my lips.

"Hush," I hissed.

The music wasn't nearly as loud as it had been on Monday, but then we weren't in the bedroom this time. Still, I could make out the melody—something sad and sweet that made goose bumps break out on my arms—and I almost held my breath, straining to hear better. I felt like I could almost recognize the song, and if I just—

"What are y'all doing?"

Ruby and I both jumped away from the door, making nearly identical yelps of surprise.

Susanna stood there, notebook in hand, frowning at us.

"Okay, *do not* sneak up on people who are listening to spooky music box sounds, Susanna," Ruby said, and Susanna raised her eyebrows at us.

"What spooky music box sounds?"

Ruby and I looked at each other. It was getting hot up here

on the second floor, the air close, still smelling like about a million years of dust had settled over the place, but even over the sound of our breathing and the muffled noises of people working downstairs, I could still hear the music. If anything, it was a little louder now, like it was out in the actual bedroom, not behind that one little door.

What was that little door, anyway? A closet?

Ruby waved at Susanna, beckoning her closer. "Listen," she said.

Susanna kept standing there, her dark eyes moving back and forth between us like she was trying to work out if this was a trick or not.

But after a second, she shrugged and walked over, placing her ear to the door.

Ruby and I scooted back to give her room, both of us on either side of her, waiting.

Then her eyes widened. "Oh, wow," she breathed, and Ruby grinned at me over the top of Susanna's head.

"I *do* hear something," Susanna went on.

Then she pulled away from the door and fixed me with a look. "I hear two jerks who think I'll fall for this."

Ruby's grin collapsed on her face. "What?"

With a scoffing sound, Susanna backed away from the door and put her hands on her hips.

"'Oooooh, we hear a spooky music box in a spooooooooky house!'" Susanna mocked, waggling her fingers at us.

Then she dropped her hands. "Please."

"This isn't a trick!" Ruby insisted, and I shook my head.

"It's really not," I said, then stepped back to the door again. "Can't you *hear* it?" I asked Susanna, because once again, it was clear as day to me, as loud as though someone were holding a music box on the other side of the door.

Ruby joined me, pressing both her palms to the wood as she leaned in.

We both stood there, ears pressed to the door, facing each other as inside the bedroom, the tune played on and on. It was going a little slower now, like it was winding down.

"It's—" I started, but Ruby nodded, finishing my thought for me.

"It's almost done."

The melody slurred and slowed, and finally, with a few more distant plinks, it faded out altogether.

Ruby and I turned to look at Susanna, who was still watching us, hands on hips, head cocked to one side.

After a second, she rolled her eyes again and, muttering something about how dumb we must think she was, turned and headed back downstairs.

Ruby and I stood there in the silent hallway. There was sweat dripping down my back, but I was still covered in goose bumps, and Ruby was fiddling with the red string bracelet around one wrist.

"That's . . . weird," she finally said, and I stepped back from the door.

"What, that we heard it, or that Susanna didn't?"

She shrugged, tucking her blue streak behind one ear. "Both, I guess. Maybe we're magic?"

I wanted to scoff at that and point out that hearing a mysterious music box didn't seem all that magical to me, but then it *was* really weird. No one had heard it the other day, either, but I'd thought maybe *I* had been mishearing things, too. There was no doubt in my mind that I'd heard the music box today, though, and I also didn't think Susanna was lying about *not* hearing it.

So what did any of that mean?

"We should explore more of the house!" Ruby suddenly said, her eyes bright. "Maybe we'll hear more creepy things!"

That sounded like the last thing in the world I wanted to do. I just wanted to go and eat my PB&J in peace and maybe see if I could get some kind of duty that kept me on the ground floor for the rest of the day.

Near the adults.

Which felt stupid and babyish, and not like something I should say out loud.

Emma would do it, I suddenly thought. Emma would have loved this, the idea that she and Ruby were hearing something, just the two of them. She would've jumped at the chance to turn this boring summer of chores into an adventure, even if she didn't really believe in this stuff.

But I wasn't Emma, and I shook my head, jerking my thumb toward the stairs.

"It's almost lunch," I said, "so I'm gonna . . . go do that."

Ruby's face didn't exactly fall, but I could tell she was disappointed. Her shoulders slumped a little.

"Okay, whatever," she said, kneeling down to tie her shoe.

I stood there awkwardly, wondering if I should wait for her to come down with me, or if she was expecting me to leave already.

And then, with a soft clicking sound, the bedroom door swung open.

Ruby and I both froze, Ruby still crouched on the ground. Her hair had swung into her face, so I couldn't see her as she said, "That door was locked."

There was no music coming from the bedroom now, but I thought I caught a faint, sort of flowery smell. Like perfume or the scented powder my grandmother bought me and Emma for Christmas.

Ruby rose to her feet and made for the door, but I found myself catching her elbow, pulling her up short.

"What are you doing?" I whispered, then realized there was no reason to be quiet.

"Um, I'm going in the room that opened up mysteriously by itself, duh," she replied, also keeping her voice low.

And when she stepped through the doorway, I found myself following her, even as I told myself that I was going to tell her to stop, that she needed to come back into the hallway and go downstairs.

But when we walked into the bedroom, the first thing I saw was the little door in the back of the room.

Open.

"Oh, man," Ruby breathed, moving closer to it. The room was hot and dim, but I fought the urge to chafe my hands up and down my arms.

There was no light in the little room, which wasn't even big enough to be a real closet, but the bedroom got enough sun for me to make out stacks of boxes against the wall and, hanging up on a rod over the jumble of stuff, two white dresses.

They hung there, looking ghostly in the dim light, and when Ruby reached out to brush a finger over the yellowing fabric, I stopped her.

"Don't," I said, even though I wasn't sure why. I was thinking of that picture downstairs, the one with the twins in their white dresses. Had these been those dresses? Was this *their* stuff in this little hidden room?

Crouching down, Ruby peered into the space, then tapped the top of my shoe. "Bingo," she said, and sure enough, a music box sat against the back wall, almost hidden in the shadows.

There was no music now as Ruby gently pulled it out of the tiny storage space. It wasn't all that fancy. I'd gotten one for my birthday a few years ago with a ballerina that twirled in front of a mirror, but this was just . . . a box. A pretty one, with designs carved on its dark wood and a yellow silk lining inside, but nothing else.

Except a key.

Ruby plucked the key up from the box. "What the what?" she muttered.

The key was big, a heavy piece of iron with rust around the teeth. The top of it was sculpted into a pretty, complicated shape, but it was only when Ruby turned the key right side up that I could see what it was.

A tree.

"It looks like the tree in the hall," Ruby said, and I shook my head, even though, to be honest, it really did. But wouldn't all big trees kind of look the same?

"What do you think—" I started.

But then, from the hall, I heard Lee call, "Ruby? Olivia?"

Ruby didn't even hesitate as she shoved the key into the back pocket of her shorts and closed the music box.

"C'mon," she whispered, then grabbed my wrist and pulled me out of the room.

Lee hadn't made it to our part of the hallway yet, so we were able to gently close the bedroom door behind us and make our way to the stairs like we'd totally been where we were supposed to be.

Lee was waiting in the middle of the staircase, one hand resting on the banister, and when he saw us, he grinned and waved. "There y'all are. Come on, lunch break!"

He turned and jogged back down the stairs, but Ruby and I stood there for a second.

"Okay, we have *got* to talk about this," Ruby said, and I glanced over my shoulder at her, then back toward where Lee had disappeared.

Ruby waved one hand. "Not here, gotcha. Here."

My notebook was still in one hand, and she took it from me, scrawling something on a page.

When I took it back, I saw *RubyToozday* written in big, bold script.

"We can chat online," she told me, nodding at her handle. "Then no one will have to know you talk to me, it's cool."

With that, she passed me and headed downstairs.

OliviaAnneWillingham: Hi.

RubyToozday: Wow, I wonder who this could be?

OliviaAnneWillingham: Haha.

RubyToozday: Seriously, didn't anyone have the Internet Stranger Danger conversation with you? You can't put your REAL name out there.

OliviaAnneWillingham: You're the only person I'm chatting to on this thing, and you already know who I am.

RubyToozday: Fair enough. We'll find you something new eventually.

RubyToozday: Do you like OliviaGarden? Like Olive Garden?

OliviaAnneWillingham: No.

RubyToozday: How about OHHHHHHLivia3000?

OliviaAnneWillingham: No.

RubyToozday: LivWhileWereYoung.

OliviaAnneWillingham: That's not grammatically correct, and NO.

OliviaAnneWillingham: And anyway, I don't want to talk about my username, I want to talk about what happened today. At the house.

RubyToozday: How I called you a liar?

RubyToozday: I stand by that, Lying Liar Who Lies.

OliviaAnneWillingham: You know what, never mind. This was a dumb idea.

RubyToozday: WAIT. Okay, I'm sorry, you're right. If you've gone to all this trouble to make a chat name, the least I can do is hear you out.

OliviaAnneWillingham: Thank you.

RubyToozday: No matter how dumb that chat name is.

RubyToozday: SORRY. DON'T GO, LET'S TALK ABOUT SPOOKY HOUSES.

OliviaAnneWillingham: I've been thinking about that key. The one we found with the music box.

RubyToozday: I knew which key you meant, COME ON. But yeah, it was weird, right? I still have it.

RubyToozday: I tried it in a few doors today, but nothing.

OliviaAnneWillingham: Yeah, but it didn't look like a key that would fit one of the doors? It's way too big.

RubyToozday: Excellent powers of observation!

RubyToozday: (I mean that, I'm not being mean.)

OliviaAnneWillingham: Thanks.

OliviaAnneWillingham: Also, it wasn't that I didn't want anyone knowing I talked to you. I just didn't want to talk about all of that there in case someone overheard us.

OliviaAnneWillingham: Susanna already thinks we're making it up.

RubyToozday: Or hallucinating from bad juice.

RubyToozday: Which, I mean, gross as the juice boxes are, I could believe it.

OliviaAnneWillingham: It's only the kiwi-strawberry that are gross. And the lemonade. The fruit punch is okay.

RubyToozday: NOW you tell me.

OliviaAnneWillingham: Anyway, why would we hear stuff? Or find a key? What's the key even for?

RubyToozday: There are stories about the place. Garrett told me something about a floating head?

RubyToozday: Floating heads seem like something worth looking into, I guess.

OliviaAnneWillingham: Maybe we should do some research.

RubyToozday: Into what? "Is this house haunted?" It CLEARLY IS. And it's super old, all super old houses are haunted.

RubyToozday: That's science.

RubyToozday: Check yo science, Liv.

OliviaAnneWillingham: I can't argue with science I guess.

OliviaAnneWillingham: Or floating heads.

RubyToozday: If you're going to make jokes, this is going to get very weird for me. I'm not prepared to deal with a Funny Olivia (Anne Willingham, Esquire).

OliviaAnneWillingham: ESQUIRE. I knew I left something off.

RubyToozday: Arrrrrggggghhhhhhh, noooooo, more funny, stop, the world is upside dooooowwwwwnnnn.

OliviaAnneWillingham: You are so weird.

OliviaAnneWillingham: Anyway, I was going to go to the bookstore on Saturday and see if there are any books about haunted houses, or even the history of Live Oak House.

OliviaAnneWillingham: Do you want to come with me?

RubyToozday: What, like together? You and me, going to the bookstore?

OliviaAnneWillingham: That's what "with" means.

RubyToozday: Sure, I'll come.

RubyToozday: But only because I think you might be a joke-making robot who replaced Olivia.

CHAPTER 14

OLIVIA

The little bookstore downtown was one of my favorite places in all of Chester's Gap. It was wedged between a boutique that mostly sold candles and local art, and another, weird little shop I'd never been into called Cosmos. The lady who ran the place did palm readings and sold incense, books on yoga, stuff like that. I wasn't sure how much business a shop like that got in our town (when it first opened, some people wanted it closed because they thought it might turn us all into witches or something), but I still liked the curtains in the window, all navy blue and printed with stars.

Mom dropped me off at Books on Main a little before eleven, reminding me to meet her by the fountain at twelve. It was only in the last year or so that me and Em had been allowed to be downtown by ourselves, but it was such a small area—just one two-lane road lined with shops, really—that there wasn't much trouble we could get into, I guess.

Chester's Gap was a small town anyway, the kind of place people moved to when they got tired of Nashville or Memphis. Mom always said it was kind of a *fake* small town. Thirty years ago, it had been a one-stoplight town with a gas station and a greasy-spoon diner, but then in the eighties, some famous country musician had dumped a bunch of money into Chester's Gap, turning it into the *idea* of Small Town, USA. Now we sold stuff with "artisan" on the label, and we had a famous Christmas parade every year that filled up the town with tourists.

Still, I liked it. Maybe it wasn't the most *genuine* town, but it was pretty and cozy. It was *home*.

I was still waiting outside Cosmos for Ruby when I felt the phone in my back pocket buzz.

Pulling it out, I saw that it was Em, trying to get me on Hangouts. My thumb hovered over the screen. I'd never *not* taken a call from her before, and it felt mean to ignore her, but at the same time, she'd ask where I was and what I was doing. She'd be able to see I was downtown, and what if Ruby came up while we were chatting? Was I ready to explain to Em that I was *willingly* spending a day with Ruby Kaye?

I didn't think I was, so after a second I slid the phone back into my pocket, which turned out to be a good idea since only a few seconds later, I saw Ruby get out of a red car a little farther down the street. She was wearing all black, her T-shirt, her shorts, her shoes, everything except her socks, which were rainbow striped. She had one tugged up nearly to her knee, the other puddled around her ankle, but it didn't seem to bug her as she jogged up.

"Oooh, are we going into the hippie store?" she asked, her eyes widening as she looked at Cosmos. "I've never been in there, and I bet they'd have stuff about hauntings."

I shook my head. "No, I told my mom we were going to Books on Main." I pointed at the store and waited for Ruby to give me a hard time about not wanting to go in Cosmos.

But she just shrugged. "Cool," she said. "Mrs. Freely said they sold that book about Live Oak House there, so that can be a start."

I had twenty dollars because Mom wanted me to pick up a book to mail to Em, too. I didn't know how much Ruby had, or even what we should look for, and for a second, we stood awkwardly on the sidewalk. It was one thing hanging out with Ruby at Camp Chrysalis, but this was us *choosing* to hang out, and even though I liked Ruby a little more than I used to, I wasn't sure this had been the best idea.

But then she turned and walked into the bookstore, and I followed.

The little bell over the door jingled as we walked in, and Ruby immediately took a deep breath. "Mmmm, Book Smell," she said happily, and I looked over at her in surprise.

"That's one of my favorite smells, too," I told her, and she wiggled her eyebrows at me.

"Well, yeah, you're a smart lady of taste and sophistication. Of course you can appreciate the greatness of Book Smell."

The store was kind of crowded, what with it being Saturday, and there were plenty of people browsing. I saw Callie from my history class last year, and Brandon, who'd been in my class all through elementary school. I waved but didn't go talk to either one of them, wanting to stay focused on today's mission. Usually, when Emma and I came into Books on Main, we headed straight for the shelves at the edge of the children's section, right under the big fake tree where they did story time for the littler kids. I wasn't even sure where to look for books on hauntings or ghosts, but Ruby edged straight past Sci-fi/Fantasy, turned right at the Romance section, and led me to a single shelf with NEW AGE printed on top in block letters.

"Here we go," she said, crouching down.

I did the same, my eyes flying over the various spines and titles. *"Tarot for Beginners,"* I read. *"The New Witch . . . Abductions: Real or Not?"*

"Real, totes," Ruby said, distracted as she scanned the shelves. "Ah!" she finally said, the bracelets on her wrist jangling as her hand shot out to pull a book from the shelf.

"Hauntings," I read, then glanced over at her. "That's pretty direct."

"And totally what we're looking for," she reminded me. "Getting right to the heart of the matter."

She started flipping through the book, and I leaned closer to read along with her. The chapter titles were all things like "Poltergeists" and "Possessions," and while those things sounded kind of interesting—okay, and also really, really terrifying and nothing I wanted to read about—I got the sense that we weren't seeing what we needed.

Ruby must've felt the same, because she shoved the book back onto the shelf and shook her head. "I don't think this one will help. Maybe we *should* try Cosmos."

Chewing my lower lip, I drummed my fingers on one of the shelves. "No, because then we'd have to talk to the lady that runs the place and actually ask for help. Here, we can just, you know. Browse. They might not even *have* books at Cosmos."

Ruby was looking at me, her head tilted a little to the side. "You don't like talking to people, do you?" she asked at last, and my face went hot.

"It's not that," I said, even though it was totally that. I snatched *Hauntings* back off the shelf, holding it against my chest. "We can start with this one, anyway."

Ruby kept looking at me, her eyes a little narrowed, but I turned away before she could say anything else, heading for the familiar shelves and looking for something Em might like.

After a second, Ruby appeared at my side, running her fingers along the spines. "It's okay if you don't like talking to people," she said. "I probably talk too much."

"You do," I told her, but she only smiled at that.

"And honestly," Ruby went on, pulling a book from the shelf, "it's nice to know you're just shy. I always thought you didn't like me and that's why you never talked to me."

I was looking at a book about a girl who falls in love with a rock star, since that seemed like Em's kind of thing, but now I looked up at Ruby, unsure of what to say exactly.

The truth was, I hadn't really liked Ruby, but was that because of *Ruby*, or because I always felt weird about how close she and Emma had gotten? "You're okay," I said to Ruby now, and she laughed, tucking her own book under her arm.

"Oh, man, Liv, don't get all gushy on me now," she said, but she bumped me a little as she walked past. It was the nice kind of bump, though, and she was still smiling.

As we made our way over to the counter, books in hand, I realized I was smiling, too.

Ruby paused in front of a little display labeled LOCAL AU-THORS. "I bet . . . ," she said, then, with an "aha," she picked up another book.

Live Oak House was on the cover, and *Live Oak: A History* was written in fancy script. The sepia-tinted picture made the house look nicer than it really was, and I wondered what it might tell us, but then Ruby turned it over, her eyebrows shooting up.

"Twenty-five dollars?" she read. "This is *robbery*."

Shaking her head, she put it back, then hefted the *Hauntings* book she'd found again. "We'll start here," she told me, "and only shell out for the fancy book if things get *bad*."

I wasn't sure I wanted to know what "bad" at Live Oak House looked like for Ruby.

CHAPTER 15

RUBY

We stood outside the bookstore, and I shaded my eyes with one hand, looking around the square. "We've still got like half an hour before we have to meet our moms," I said to Liv as she shifted her bag from one side to the other. "So we could go get yogurt? I have money left over."

"So do I," Olivia replied, looking over at Yo Yo Yo, the frozen yogurt place across the way. There were like a million frozen yogurt places in Chester's Gap now, but this one was my favorite because it was so close to the bookstore. Grammy used to take me over there after we'd do our shopping, and once again, thinking of her made something in my throat feel tight. I wondered if you ever stopped missing people, if stupid little things like frozen yogurt places ever stopped stinging.

Before I could do something dumb like tear up, I waved at Olivia with one arm. "C'mon," I said, and made a dash for it even though there were no cars coming and the crosswalk was only a few feet away.

Liv, of course, walked down there, pressed the button, and

waited for the light, so I stood on the other side, waiting on her with my arms crossed and an exaggerated expression of impatience on my face.

"There's no one coming!" I hollered.

But she held her bag and called back, "Waiting a minute or two could be the difference between life and death, Ruby!"

I couldn't tell if she was joking—that did kind of sound like something Olivia would say in total seriousness—but then she grinned at me, and a few seconds before the light changed, she darted across the street.

There were still no cars coming, but I widened my eyes at her. "Living dangerously, girl!"

She laughed again, shaking her head, and then walked past me toward Yo Yo Yo.

A blast of air-conditioning hit us as we walked into the yogurt shop, the smell of chocolate and waffle cones and all other things that are good and amazing in this world wafting toward me.

There was a bored teenager behind the register who barely looked up at us as Liv put her bag of books on the table and we went to go grab our cups. I got the medium-sized one since I had a ten left over from the bookstore, and when you have a chance to get as much frozen yogurt as you want, you should really go big or go home. I noticed that Olivia got one of the smaller ones, but that wasn't exactly a surprise.

I walked over to the row of yogurt machines, holding my cup in both hands. Picking out the right combo of flavors was crucial to the whole yogurt experience, and Yo Yo Yo had at least sixteen flavors. Looking over, I saw Liv already sitting back down, her yogurt cup in front of her, and not even filled up all that high. I couldn't see any sprinkles or whipped cream or anything.

Frowning, I looked back at the machines, finally settling on a mix of vanilla, salted caramel, and white chocolate. That done, I loaded on a Willy Wonka's Chocolate Factory amount of toppings, paid at the counter, and then sat down across from Olivia.

Sure enough, her yogurt was totally boring: their "house" flavor, which tasted like actual yogurt, a handful of strawberries, some bright green kiwi pieces, and a few bits of granola.

"That's the saddest frozen yogurt I've ever seen," I told her, and she licked her neon-orange spoon before wrinkling her nose at me.

"It's good," she said. "And I always get the healthy one."

I raised my eyebrows, digging my own spoon into the sugary masterpiece I'd created. "What does that mean?"

Olivia's face went a little pink and she ducked her head, using the tip of her spoon to cut part of the kiwi slice.

"Emma," she said, like that explained everything.

It probably did, to her. Em used to do the same thing when she talked about Olivia sometimes, like just saying her name could conjure up all the reasons she might do or say something. Maybe that's what it's like when you're a twin—you know those things about each other.

But I didn't know, so I took a bite of yogurt and said, "Explain."

Olivia looked up at the ceiling for a second. "Just that . . . whenever we get frozen yogurt, I get the healthy one, and Em gets the . . . well, one like that, and we share. It's a thing."

I thought about that for a second. "Do you want to share?" I asked, and she actually blushed a deeper red, shaking her head, her blond hair sweeping her shoulders.

"No, I was just telling you why I got this yogurt."

"Okay," I replied, and then we were quiet again.

Yo Yo Yo wasn't that crowded, only one other family at a polka-dotted plastic table, and the big-screen TV on the far wall was showing the Food Network, some older lady with dark hair smiling way too much as she sliced some hard-boiled eggs.

I dug around in my yogurt some more before saying, "Does Emma ever get the healthy one, or just you?"

Olivia clearly wanted nothing more than for this conversation to end, because she practically waved me off with her spoon.

"No, just me. It's stupid, we probably shouldn't even do it anymore."

I could've let it drop, but I felt like there was something important about this yogurt thing.

"Do you want to swap?" I said, and Liv looked up, her green eyes narrowing.

"What?"

"You can have this yogurt, and I'll take yours. Then you can be the one who gets the awesome, rad yogurt that is prepared like yogurt was meant to be, and I can be the person who gets the sad yogurt."

She frowned at me. "This isn't sad yogurt."

"It's so sad, Liv. It's the saddest yogurt in all the land. It makes a journal about its sad feelings and listens to sad music while crying. Sadly."

The corners of her mouth started turning up a little bit. "Okay, you've made your point—"

"That yogurt writes poems about how sad it is, Liv. Its favorite color is blue because blue is the saddest color."

She was giggling now, and after a second, she reached over and dug her spoon into my yogurt, managing to pull out a bite of cookie dough, sprinkles, and whipped cream.

Watching me, she shoved the whole thing into her mouth. "Oh, wow," she said around a mouthful, and I laughed.

"See, that's happy yogurt," I told her. "Which you might not recognize, since it actually tastes like food."

"It doesn't taste like food," she said, shaking her head. And then she grinned. "It tastes like *joy*."

I laughed again, and we abandoned her healthy sad yogurt altogether, both of us sharing mine. Once we'd scraped the bottom of the cup, we sat there for a moment in silence, until Olivia patted the bag of books.

"Do you really think there's anything good in here?" she asked, and I shrugged.

"It's worth a try. And my mom said she'd take me to the library next weekend, so I'll look there, too."

Olivia's spoon was empty, but she tapped it against her lips anyway, thinking. "Haunted houses aren't exactly rare," she mused. "Which means there has to be something somewhere that could help."

I wrinkled my nose at her. "Help?"

Dropping her spoon, Liv raised her eyebrows at me. "Well,

yeah. Why else would we be doing all this research about a haunted house if we weren't gonna, you know, de-haunt it?"

"Ohhhh, Liv," I sighed. "Ohhhhhhhlivia." And she picked up a stray sprinkle from the table and flicked it at me.

I dodged, giggling, but still said, "We can't fix it. We can just, you know, understand what it is. Know what we're up against and how to best keep ourselves non-ghost-smacked for the rest of the summer. I'm not about to go full-on Ghostbuster at Live Oak House."

"So this isn't about helping, it's about understanding," she said slowly, thinking that over, and while that wasn't exactly what I'd meant—really, this was mostly a fun distraction from cleaning that stupid place—I nodded.

"Yeah, exactly."

She tilted her head to one side, tapping her spoon to her mouth again, then gave a sharp nod. "Okay. I like that. Like we're not ghost *hunters*, but ghost *researchers*. Town historians, even!"

Liv said that so brightly that I made myself smile at her even though "town historian" was not a title I ever really wanted, thanks.

"So next thing we need to do," I said, "is explore more of the house. Find out where that key goes."

Nodding, Liv cleaned up a stray spot of melted yogurt with her napkin. "Explore more of the house," she repeated. "But Mrs. Freely said it's not all safe."

"Mrs. Freely also said there was nothing spooky happening at the house, and we know *that's* not true," I countered. "And, I mean, if she's telling the truth and we fall through a floor or something, at least our parents can sue, and then we can buy a boat or something." I reached across the table to poke her with my spoon. "Bright side, Liv!"

She didn't seem all that convinced, but she still said, "So where should we start on Monday, then?"

That was the spirit. Grinning, I reached over to her sad yogurt to scoop a stray bit of kiwi off the top. "The only place I can think where that key might fit," I told her, and when she looked at me, confused, I leaned closer and whispered, "The attic."

CHAPTER 16

OLIVIA

"**D**id you have fun?"

As I buckled my seat belt, I shrugged at Mom. I *did* have fun today, which was . . . kind of unexpected, but I wasn't sure I was ready to tell Mom that. It wasn't like Ruby and I were becoming friends, after all. We were like . . . coworkers, I guess. Making the best out of the summer, and now trying to figure out what was going on at Live Oak House.

That was another thing I didn't want to get into with Mom: the weirdness of Live Oak House. The music box and the key were . . . odd, for sure. Something I couldn't explain. But there was a part of me thinking there had to be some explanation other than "ghosts," and an even tinier, sadder part of me that worried that this was all some kind of prank Ruby had put together.

But she'd been nice to me at the bookstore, nice at the yogurt place, and kind of fun to hang out with. It had been a long time since I'd spent time with another girl my age who wasn't Emma. One of the things with twins, I guess—the built-in best friend thing.

Turning off of Main Street and back toward the road that led to Chester's Gap's suburbs, Mom glanced over at me.

"I thought we might try to see if Em wanted to Skype in for dinner tonight. We'd have to eat a little later if we want to match up with her time at camp, but it could be fun, huh?"

"Did you run that by Em?" I asked, and Mom shook her head, signaling a left turn.

"I was going to have you ask on the . . . the phone thingie when we got home."

I smiled at that. "Hangouts," I corrected, and Mom gave a nod.

"Hangouts, right."

We were quiet for a little while, and then Mom said, "I know you miss her a lot."

I suddenly wanted to fidget in my seat, and to keep from doing that, I leaned forward, changing the radio station. "Yeah, but we talk. On the phone and stuff. It's fine."

Sighing, Mom reached out and covered my hand, keeping me from pushing any more buttons.

"Livvy, I know we haven't really talked about what happened, but that's because I was hoping you might come to me." She smiled, cutting her eyes at me briefly before turning back to the road. "You can be tough to crack sometimes, you know that? Like . . . an oyster."

It was such a weird image that I laughed a little. "I'm an oyster?"

Mom nodded, turning onto our street, a sprinkler spraying the side of the car as she did. Our neighbors were really serious about their yards.

"Emma is an open book with what she's feeling. She can never really keep a secret, even though she sure does try sometimes. But you? You hold everything really close inside. And that can be good!"

We were in our driveway now, and while Mom put the car in park, she didn't turn it off.

"It means you're trustworthy," she went on, "and that you ... you put value on your feelings. But sometimes I think you could open up just a little bit more, sweetie."

There was a squirming feeling inside my stomach, and I suddenly felt like I might cry or something. Mom was like Emma—when she felt things, she said them. I felt things, too, but when it came to talking about them, it seemed too hard. Like I had to say what I was feeling and then explain it, too, just in case what I was feeling was wrong, or—

Mom smoothed my hair down, her palm warm on the back of my head. "I only want you to know you can talk to me, Livvy. About anything."

I looked up at her then, and I knew. I *knew* she knew who really took that lipstick.

That she'd probably known from the very first day. And I wanted to tell her about it then, I really did. Let the whole thing spill out, messy as it was, about how I'd done it to save Emma, but also to test her, maybe, and was that something that was okay to do? To make people who love you prove it?

But before I could say anything, my phone blooped.

Emma.

Smiling, Mom turned off the car and opened her door. "Ask her about dinner," she said, and then she was sliding out, leaving me alone in the car.

Taking a deep breath, I answered the call, Emma's face filling my screen immediately.

"There you are!" she said, grinning. Then she leaned in so close, her face went blurry. "Where were you?"

"I went to the bookstore," I told her, and she leaned back, her face coming back into focus.

"Oh, yay! Did you get me anything?"

"A book of poetry all about trees," I told her, and she scowled. "Seriously?"

I pulled my feet up onto the edge of the car seat, resting my arms on my knees and holding the phone a little closer to my face. "No, Em, not seriously. I got you some book about a girl who dates this singer guy."

"Whew," Em said, leaning back. "That's more like it."

I frowned at the tiny screen, wishing I could see more of where Emma was. It looked like she was sitting outside her cabin. The light was bright, and I could make out the log wall behind her.

"Did you honestly think I'd get you a book of tree poems?"

Em's eyes darted somewhere beyond her phone, like there was someone else standing nearby, and I pulled the phone even closer, like if I did, I'd be able to see better.

"There's no telling with you, Livvy," she said, and one corner of her mouth kicked up, the dimple we both had appearing in her cheek.

I still had the uncomfortable feeling she wasn't alone, and I didn't like that, talking in front of other people. Still, I went on. "Oh, speaking of trees, there's this *crazy* one at Live Oak House. Like, this massive tree trunk in the middle of—"

Emma suddenly burst out laughing and I sat back, confused. "What?"

Shaking her head, Emma covered her mouth with one hand, the phone shaking slightly. "It's not you, Livvy, it's just Sasha being an idiot."

I didn't know who Sasha was, so I gave a weak "Okay."

Em's eyes met mine again, and she shrugged. "It's so hard to talk around here, and we're about to go to archery. Can I call you later?"

You called me, I wanted to remind her. *Twice.*

Instead, I nodded. "Yeah, sure."

"Thanks, Livvy! Love you!" she said, waggling her fingers.

Her face blipped out, and it was only as I was headed back into the house that I remembered I'd forgotten to ask her about dinner.

CHAPTER 17

RUBY

Sneaking into the attic was tougher than I'd thought it would be.

That Monday, Liv and I volunteered to work together, cataloging the stuff in that room we'd seen the first day with all the paintings.

I'd purposely picked the room because I'd noticed last week that while Mrs. Freely, Lee, and Leigh checked on us regularly, they sometimes forgot about the back of the house on their rotations. Hardly anyone checked on me and Garrett the same way they checked the rest of the group, and that meant that me and Liv might have some time before anyone realized we'd gone missing.

So sneaking out and toward the stairs that led to the attic wasn't the hard part.

Liv was the hard part.

"Maybe we should skip this," she said to me as we counted the pictures in that room. That was my idea—if Mrs. Freely asked us what had taken so long back here, we could pretend we'd misunderstood and just *counted* pictures instead of listing them. I thought she might actually buy it, and was pretty proud of myself for coming up with it.

But Liv was sitting on the floor under the chair rail, her legs crossed, the eraser of her pencil against her teeth. She was right by the photograph she'd spotted the first day, the one with the dark-haired twins from the early 1900s. She kept glancing over at it, and I wondered if she was thinking about Emma.

Then I wondered if I should ask her. I was still curious about why Olivia was here, and I was convinced it had something to do with Emma. But if Liv wanted to talk about it, she would, I guess.

Besides, we had a mission.

"Look, Liv," I told her now, setting my notebook down. "We heard a magic music box, which led us to a magic key, and I would bet anything that that key fits the attic, because that's how this kind of thing goes. And *that* means we owe it to ourselves to go check out the attic."

Olivia chewed on her bottom lip, and I saw her eyes flick to the picture on the wall. I really thought she was going to chicken out again, but instead, she gave a firm nod and rose to her feet.

"Okay."

In my house, the attic door was set up in the ceiling with a little string you had to pull to open it. But in Live Oak House, the attic had its own normal door up a high, narrow staircase at the back of the house, and we made our way there as quietly as we could. We were both holding our notebooks and pencils. I'd told her we should take them because then if we got caught, we'd have *plausible deniability*. Grammy had taught me that term—it meant that if you had to lie about a thing, people would believe you more because you'd prepared for it. Or something. Anyway, having our notebooks seemed like a good idea.

Another good idea? The little flashlight I'd sneaked into my pocket before leaving the house that morning.

"Just . . . if we get caught . . . ," Liv said now, and I sighed.

"What exactly are we doing that's so bad?" I asked her as we reached the door that led to the attic steps. "We're familiarizing ourselves with the house, seeing if there are any bits that require our attention." I held up my notebook, shaking it at her. "Responsible."

We crept up the stairs, the boards creaking under our feet. It was so narrow that we had to walk one at a time, Liv right behind me, and then there, at the top, was the door.

It looked heavier than the other doors in the house for some reason, thicker and stronger. There was a little window in the top, though, and light shone behind it. That made me feel better, knowing there were apparently windows inside.

I took the key out of my pocket, and it sat, heavy and cold, in my palm. There was a part of me that honestly believed the key wouldn't fit, that this was a dumb idea of mine, or even that someone was playing a prank on us. I wasn't sure *how*, but Michael and Dalton had already proven themselves to be jerks, Wesley was weird, and Garrett was . . . well, I wasn't sure, but I couldn't pretend this sort of elaborate prank wasn't out of character for him.

But the key slid into the lock easily, and when I turned it, there was a loud clicking noise.

Olivia and I looked at each other. She had her hair down today, pushed back from her face with a blue and green plaid headband that clashed with her Camp Chrysalis shirt, and I paused, wondering if she was going to call it all off again.

She didn't, though. In fact, she actually reached past me to push the door open on her own.

And then we stepped into the attic.

It was bigger than I'd expected, but then I was used to our little attic that mostly held only Christmas decorations and a few old toys that I hadn't wanted to get rid of. But this? This place was half the size of my house, I was pretty sure, and compared to the rest of Live Oak House, it actually seemed sort of empty. There were a few trunks—one of which was covered in a pile of old coats—some big garbage bags full of things, and a few old, broken pieces of furniture.

"I guess everything worth keeping is down in the house," I said, my voice sounding too loud in the quiet, dusty space.

"Maybe," Olivia agreed. "So . . . now what?"

The attic was so massive that I wasn't even sure where we should start. Or what I was looking for, to be honest. But the key had to mean something, right?

"It's actually kind of nice up here," Liv said, and I turned to see her walking toward the little circle window at the other end of the attic. I wondered who had spent so much time making that window for this space where no one would ever really see it. The panes were designed to look like the bloom of a flower, the glass in the center tinted a watery yellow, and when the sunlight hit it just right, it made prisms on the hardwood floors.

The attic was dusty and hot and dim, so I wasn't sure I would go so far as to call it "pretty," but I appreciated Liv's enthusiasm. It was one of the things I was starting to like about Olivia, really, the way she could find something nice about nearly everything— even the attic of a haunted house.

There was no need for the flashlight after all, so I kept it in my pocket and walked over to Liv. From this high up, you could actually make out the outskirts of town. I could see the very top of the Baptist church's bell tower, plus the long line of oaks that made up the main street through the historic center.

"You're right," I said, surprised. "This is nice. If I were a ghost, this is where I would stay. Take in the views, occasionally creep people out . . ."

Liv scrunched up her face at that, but at least she didn't tell me not to mention ghosts. I figured that was progress.

"But let's be real," I told her, touching her elbow lightly. "This is like the *least* spooky place we've seen in the house so far. Maybe we should go—"

My words disappeared in the loud *crack!* of the attic door suddenly slamming closed.

"Oh, no, no, no," I babbled, rushing forward, Olivia right behind me.

I had heard the heavy metallic thump of the key as it had fallen out of the door on the other side. Where I'd left it, like a total idiot.

"No, no, bad door, bad!" I continued, my fingers closing around the doorknob. It was icy cold against my hand, the kind of cold so sharp it nearly burns, and I released it with a cry. What the heck? But then I gritted my teeth and tugged again, still hoping in some little (and stupid, I guess) part of my heart that the door would just . . . give. Open.

But of course, it was shut—and locked—tight.

I kicked at the bottom of the door even though that was also stupid, but I didn't want to say a bad word in front of Liv, despite all the bad words I had ever thought of currently bashing around in my brain.

"Maybe it's stuck," Liv offered, tugging at the doorknob herself. "And if we pull hard enough . . ."

She pulled with everything she had. I could see the strain in her arms as she leaned back away from the door, both hands wrapped around the knob. She pulled hard enough that for a second I worried she'd pop the knob right off, and *then* where would we be?

Stumbling away from the door, Liv grunted and wiped her hands on her shorts.

"So, not stuck," she said, and I shook my head.

"Nope. Ghost-locked."

Liv shot me a look. "Or an old door that got caught in a draft and accidentally locked," she said, and I crossed my arms over my chest, looking down my nose at her.

"Liv," I said. "Are you honestly still doing, 'It was just some random noises! A trick of the light! Magical wind that magically locked a magical door!'"

She mimicked my pose. "Someone has to be the sensible one here, Ruby," she said, "and it's obviously never going to be you. You got us locked in the attic!"

"How is this my fault?" I asked, throwing up my hands. "I was over there with you by the window, so it's not like I'm the one who slammed the door."

"But we wouldn't be up here if it weren't for you," Liv said, pointing a finger at me. Not even pointing, really, more like stabbing the air, and I did *not* appreciate that.

"You agreed we should come up here," I shot back. "I was *trying* to help you."

Liv made a scoffing sound, blowing out her breath and ruffling her bangs. "Some help," she said. "You just—"

And then there was another sound from the opposite side of the attic, a sort of slithery thump that startled us both.

It was the trunk with all the coats on it. Those coats were now on the floor, and Liv and I glanced at each other.

"Another draft?" I asked her, and while she scowled at me, she didn't say anything. So I walked over to the trunk and knelt down, grimacing as my bare knees met the gritty floor.

"What are you doing?" Olivia asked as I lifted the lid. It gave with a creak and a shower of rust flakes.

"What does it look like?" I asked her. "Clearly whatever led us up here wants us to look in the trunk."

I waited for Olivia to say there was nothing up here, that this was all clearly some kind of joke being played on us, but instead, she crossed the attic and sat down next to me. "What's in it?"

I reached inside, pulling out a swath of fabric. Once upon a time, it had probably been white, but age had turned it yellow, and there were holes all through it.

"Ick," I muttered, tossing it aside, but Olivia caught it and gently laid it in her lap.

Under the fabric was another coat, this one heavy black wool, and under that, there were a bunch of old photographs.

"Rejects from the room downstairs?" I wondered, picking them up. There were all black-and-white, the edges wrinkled. The top one showed a family, Mom, Dad, daughter, and two babies all swaddled up, posed in front of a cabin.

Olivia tapped the babies. "I wonder if those are the twins from downstairs."

"Probably," I said, then turned the picture over.

The Wrexhall Family, 1890.

Flipping the picture back over, I studied the people in it. "That's weird," I said. "They all have dark hair."

Olivia, whose own hair was nearly as blond as Felix Wrexhall's in that portrait, was still staring at the photograph. "What does that have to do with anything?"

I moved to the next photograph in the stack. The twins again, younger than they were in the picture downstairs, but not babies anymore. Maybe about five, both sitting in front of a tree, two dolls lying on the blanket in front of them. Their older sister, the same dark-haired girl from the earlier picture, was leaning against the trunk. She looked familiar to me somehow, but I couldn't quite place her.

"The blond hair," I reminded Olivia, distracted by those dolls in the picture. Were they in the doll room downstairs? "Mrs. Freely said it was a Wrexhall family trait. These people don't have it."

Olivia leaned closer, her hair falling over her shoulders. "Maybe she was wrong? Felix and Matthew were the only Wrexhalls in this town. Maybe the ones before them had dark hair."

"Maybe," I said, but I kept looking at the pictures, thinking there was something I should be seeing, or something I was missing.

I turned this one over, and there, in pencil, was written, *Lucy with Rebecca and Octavia, 1895.*

"Lucy," Olivia said. "That was Felix's wife, right?"

Nodding, I looked closer at the picture. Lucy was standing right behind the twins, a dark shape on the blanket near her foot.

"Is that the music box?" I asked Olivia, tapping at the picture. It was hard to tell—the box could've been anything, after all, but we'd found it in Lucy's bedroom. Had it been hers or the twins'? And were they her sisters? They must've been.

"These pictures have to be important," I said to Liv, moving on to the next one. This was just of a tree, but a really big one.

Not any tree, either. I was pretty sure I was looking at the same tree that was downstairs, the big one Felix Wrexhall had had planted in the house when he built it.

Liv's fingers suddenly dug into my arm, and, irritated, I tried to shake her off.

"Yeah, yeah, I know, it's the tree," I said, but then she was standing up, tugging me so hard that I had no choice but to stand up, too.

I raised my head to see Olivia looking at something over my shoulder, her eyes wide.

"What?" I asked, and she raised one hand, pointing behind me.

"Okay, that is seriously not cool," I told her, swatting at her hand. "Don't do the 'ooooooh, there's something behiiiiind yoooouuu' thing, when—"

Without saying a word, Liv grabbed my shoulders and slowly spun me to face the attic door.

CHAPTER 18

OLIVIA

Ruby and I stood there, frozen in place, watching the top of the attic door.

Earlier, when we'd come in, I'd noticed the little window on top of the door, remembering that it was called a transom, because my parents had had one put in over our front door a few years ago so we'd have more light at the front of the house. This window didn't let in any light from the dim staircase outside, but there was something moving against it now, something darker than the gloom outside the attic.

It was more solid than I would've thought a shadow could be. And it was moving back and forth against the glass.

The glass that was at least nine feet above the floor.

And then I realized that, no, it wasn't *a* shadow.

It was *two* shadows.

Ruby was breathing slowly next to me, in and out, and when I looked over, I could see little puffs coming from her lips. Earlier, the attic had been so hot, I hadn't been sure how we could spend longer than five minutes in it, but now I was freezing, almost shivering with cold.

"You want to call that a trick of the light?" Ruby asked, and I shook my head slowly, my eyes still locked on . . . whatever it was.

There was no sound, and for some reason, that freaked me out the most. The shadows were sliding back and forth across the glass, pressing in in places, but totally noiseless. Back and forth, back and forth they went, like they were watching us, but also . . . taunting us or something.

I felt Ruby's fingers squeeze mine, and I looked down. I hadn't even realized we were holding hands, and I wasn't sure which one of us had grabbed the other. In any case, I squeezed back.

The black spots at the window seemed to stretch, growing so that they covered the whole window, and I made a weird sound in the back of my throat, stepping back and tugging Ruby with me.

And then the shadows were gone.

The window was still dim—not much light in the hall—but those darker, blacker shadows had vanished. I let out a slow breath. "Well, that—" I started, and before I could finish, there was a slam as the door shot open so hard, it smacked into the wall, making me and Ruby both jump and shriek.

It was hot in the attic again, with that same dusty smell we'd noticed when we first came in, and no trace of the chill in the air we'd felt.

I expected Ruby to be excited or say something about sticking around for more proof, but instead, she raced for her plastic caddy, snatching it up off the floor so quickly that the bottles nearly fell out, and rushed back toward me, holding her free hand out, tugging me with her. "We're getting out of here," she said, almost breathless as she pulled me out of the attic, grabbing the key as we passed the door.

We were just clomping down the stairs back to the third floor when Mrs. Freely appeared on the landing. As soon as she saw us, she stopped, hands on her hips.

"What are you two doing?"

I'm not going to lie—I came close to spilling everything right then, I was so freaked out. It will sound stupid, but somewhere in my head, I was thinking that maybe telling a grown-up about the attic and what we saw would make it feel less scary. Because she would've said something reasonable about shadows and light or something, and while I wouldn't have believed her at first, before long, I would have started accepting it, and by Friday, I'd probably be convinced I hadn't seen anything scary at all.

But before I could say anything, Ruby blurted out, "We were familiarizing ourselves with the house, Mrs. Freely. You know, making sure we knew where everything was, but in a team, so we wouldn't get lost."

Mrs. Freely tilted her head, looking down at us. "I thought the two of you didn't want to be a team," she said. "That you couldn't work together without fighting."

Ruby had dropped my hand when we got to the bottom of the stairs, but now she took it again, giving me a smile that was way too bright and way too fake. "We've overcome our differ-ences, Mrs. Freely," she said sweetly. "Learned to work together like Camp Chrysalis wants."

If Mrs. Freely hadn't been staring at us, I would've rolled my eyes. For someone so good at lying when she wanted to be, Ruby was laying it on really thick right then.

But weirdly enough, it was working. Mrs. Freely seemed to relax a little, some of the tension leaving her shoulders.

"Well, that is good," she said slowly, looking at our joined hands. "But you know you're not supposed to go above the second floor. This house is in good shape, structurally, but it's always better to be safe than sorry."

"Agreed," Ruby said, finally letting go of my hand. "In fact, I think I'll make that my first tattoo. Thanks, Mrs. Freely."

Mrs. Freely did that thing she did a lot with Ruby, blinking and jerking her head back so that she suddenly had like four chins. Not for the first time, I wondered where Ruby had learned to talk to grown-ups like that. Like she was one of them. Was it something she could teach me, or had she just been born with it?

Finally, Mrs. Freely just shook her head, sighed, and said, "Well, good. And you both might want to remember that should there be any . . . incidents here at Camp Chrysalis, there will be consequences."

I knew we had to get through the summer and "graduate" at the end, but this was the first time I'd heard about what might happen if we got in trouble *at* camp. Wasn't camp punishment enough?

But then Mrs. Freely added, "I don't like to bring it up unless I think I need to, because, of course, we want you all to be on your best behavior without any sort of . . . *negativity* hanging over you. But without a good report from me, other corrective measures might need to be taken. Detention at your school, other forms of community service . . ."

She trailed off, then smiled at both of us, patting our shoulders. "But it's not going to come to that, is it, girls?"

Swallowing hard, I shook my head, visions of picking up trash in the park suddenly all I could see. "No, ma'am," I said, even as I felt Ruby look over at me. "It's not."

CHAPTER 19

RUBY

I t had taken a while for us to figure out our lunch spots, but it eventually ended up being those two boys from the county over—Dalton and Michael—sitting under the tree together while Garrett, Liv, Wesley, Susanna, and I all sat on the porch that Friday, eating our sandwiches and drinking the bad juice boxes. Since Olivia had told me that the fruit punch was where it was at, I'd made sure to grab one for all of us as soon as I could, sometimes before it was even time for lunch. That meant that the juice was usually kind of warm before we got to it, but hey, at least it wasn't gross.

Let the Greene County guys have the icky juice.

"I am so sick of dead birds," Susanna said, tugging a corner of Swiss cheese off her sandwich and popping it in her mouth. "I'm running out of ways to list them."

"Same," Garrett said. "Well, not birds, but pictures. Still boring, though."

Wesley didn't say anything. To be honest, I'm not sure he knew how to talk, since we'd never heard him speak, but he gave a shrug that seemed to say that everything had been pretty dull for him, too. "Good point, Wes," I said, and he grinned at me from underneath his curtain of hair.

I munched on my sandwich, a creation my mom made for me involving Nutella, bananas, and a sprinkling of wheat germ. So far, Liv and I hadn't said anything to the others about the attic or the pictures, the shadows, any of it. Susanna knew about the music box, but since she hadn't heard anything, she clearly thought we were making it all up. Plus, I wasn't sure I *wanted* the others to know. It was kind of nice, having it just be me and Liv's thing. Like the house had chosen *us* for some reason.

Which probably should've been creepy but, instead, felt kind of cool.

So, no, I wasn't going to bring up the ghost stuff with the others. Instead, I tucked the rest of my sandwich back into my plastic bag, dusting my hands on my knees. "Okay," I said. "I think it's time we all fessed up to what we're here for. I'll go first. I'm Ruby Kaye, and I threw a bunch of glitter in the halls of a school. I know, I know. Totally a victimless crime."

Susanna gave me a look. "Not for the janitor," she reminded me, and I had to acknowledge that was a direct hit.

"Fair point. So why are you here?"

Sighing, Susanna sat up a little, linking her fingers on her knee. "I hit a kid with a lunch tray."

Okay, that was impressive.

Garrett snorted. "Remind me never to make you mad."

Susanna lifted one shoulder in a sort of elegant shrug. "He

was being rude to a friend of mine, and we told him to stop. He didn't stop, so. Lunch tray."

"So you're here for a noble cause. Well done, Susanna. Garrett, what—"

"I stole a lipstick," Olivia interrupted.

I swiveled my head toward her, but she was looking down again, picking at her sandwich.

"What?" I said, genuinely shocked. Olivia Anne Willingham, shoplifter? I just . . . could not see that.

She kept tearing off little bits of the crust of her PB&J, her face as pink as the bow holding back her hair today. "It was dumb, I know."

Then she raised her head, nodding at Garrett. "Sorry, your turn."

I wanted to ask her more about the lipstick. How had a girl who freaked out every time me and Emma even *thought* about breaking a rule—

Oh.

Emma.

But before I could blurt out my suspicions, Garrett was talking. "Borrowed someone's skateboard."

"Borrowed?" Susanna asked, raising an eyebrow in a way that really impressed me. I'd never been able to do just one.

Garrett pushed his hair out of his face. "I was going to bring it back, promise."

I looked over at Wesley.

"What about you?" I asked, even though I didn't really expect an answer. He'd probably just shrug or something.

But then he said, in a surprisingly deep voice, "Nothing better to do."

We all took that in, and finally, I shook my head and said, "Okay, cool, so Wes is clearly the weirdest among us."

He grinned at that, because he *was* the weirdest among us, and then, almost as one, the five of us turned to look at the two other boys, Michael and Dalton.

"What do we think they did?" I asked, and Susanna narrowed her eyes.

"Michael goes to my school," she said, "and I think he probably got in a fight or something. He does that a lot. The other one, who knows?"

"Various Jerkery," I said, remembering how mean he'd been about Olivia's journal, and the others all laughed.

Lunch was nearly over by then, and we all started picking up our trash and heading back inside.

As we did, I hung back near Liv, and only when the others had walked off did I ask, "So it was Emma, right?"

Olivia turned to me, her eyes wide, and I was glad she didn't pretend not to know what I was talking about.

"Emma took the lipstick, and you took the fall?" I went on, and after a second, she shook her head.

"I know," she said, and she sounded so . . . sad. "It was dumb."

"Not dumb," I said, and I kind of wanted to put an arm around her shoulders or something, but I didn't. "Just . . . being a good sister."

Liv looked at me for a long time, a little wrinkle between

her eyebrows, and I could tell she was trying to decide if I was being serious or not.

So then I *did* put an arm around her shoulders, steering her to face Michael and Dalton just as Dalton tried to flip his water bottle into the big trash can Mrs. Freely had set up outside.

The bottle flipped all right, but it hit the edge of the trash can, splashing water back onto Dalton, who spluttered and said a word that would've gotten him in big trouble if Mrs. Freely had heard him.

"See that?" I told Liv. "*That* is dumb."

She made a sort of choking sound that turned into a laugh, and as we walked back into the house, I kept my arm around her.

RubyToozday: I've been thinking!

OliviaAnneWillingham: Dangerous.

RubyToozday: RUDE.

RubyToozday: About the house. All the stuff we've seen so far, the music box in that weird little closet, the pictures, the shadows, it all has to fit together somehow, right?

RubyToozday: Unless you think the house is just FULL OF GHOSTS.

OliviaAnneWillingham: No, I was thinking that, too. It means something, right?

OliviaAnneWillingham: Maybe the twins? Those little girls in the picture?

OliviaAnneWillingham: The music box was in that picture. We saw their dresses in that closet.

RubyToozday: And twins are creepy.

RubyToozday: No offense.

OliviaAnneWillingham: None taken. They were with Lucy in that picture, right?

OliviaAnneWillingham: They must've been her sisters.

OliviaAnneWillingham: But everyone says Lucy and Felix didn't have family.

RubyToozday: And why would Lucy's little sisters be haunting a place where they didn't even live?

RubyToozday: Ghosts are weird, man.

OliviaAnneWillingham: You're weird.

RubyToozday: RUDE AGAIN SOME MORE.

CHAPTER 20

RUBY

"I cannot believe we're being entrusted with this," I said that Monday, looking down at the paint buckets in front of us.

It's not that I wasn't excited about having something *new* to do, something that was not logging things in a notebook, but painting? Who gave a bunch of kids *paint* and said, "Go at it"?

I'd asked Mrs. Freely that, and she'd said this was a "base coat" and that professional painters would do the real work, and then, when I wondered out loud if maybe Mrs. Freely was just running out of stuff for us to do, she did that pressed lips/closed eyes thing again.

But now Garrett and I were in one of the second-floor bedrooms, three open cans of paint in front of us, staring at the blank walls.

"I don't know, I think I might have some hidden artistic talent," Garrett said, squatting down to dip his brush into the paint.

He rose back up, grinned at me, and gave the brush a little spin, and I guess that would've been cute if the paint hadn't splattered him, me, and the wall in front of us.

"Awesome," I muttered, looking at the splashes of Eggshell Sunlight on my bright pink shirt.

"Sorry," he said, sheepish. Or as sheepish as Garrett got, I guess, since he added, "But it's not like paint makes these shirts any uglier."

"Sad, but true," I answered, and then looked back at the wall. Would a coat of paint make it less horror-movie-set-looking? I was not convinced, but then, painting was a lot more fun than cleaning, so I was willing to give it a shot.

There was a bump from behind us, and we both turned to see Liv coming in, her own bucket of paint clutched in one hand, a paintbrush in the other. She was wearing her hair in a braid as usual, but there was a hot-pink ribbon twisted in it to match her shirt. A few weeks ago, that bright pink ribbon would have irritated me, but today, it made me smile and think that hey, at least she was making the best out of a terrible outfit.

"Do you think this is safe?" she asked, looking up at me and Garrett with a frown. "Letting us paint? This room doesn't seem all that ventilated."

Ah, there was the Olivia who irritated me. "They wouldn't let us do it if it wasn't safe," I reasoned, dipping my brush into Garrett's open can of paint. "Because illegal."

"I feel like all of this probably violates some kind of child labor law," Garrett said with a shrug. "But they made our parents sign a ton of paperwork before we even got here, so . . ."

He let that trail off, and Olivia and I looked at each other.

"Our parents wouldn't let us do something that wasn't safe," she finally said in that "I am Olivia Anne Willingham, and my word is law" tone, and then she dipped her own brush into the paint and smoothed a solid stripe on the wall.

"Your faith is touching, Liv," I told her, but I started painting, too, and for a while we worked quietly. It was actually kind of nice, not having to fill up the silence. I liked to talk—probably too much—maybe because the house was so quiet in the afternoons now that I was staying by myself and not with Grammy anymore. But then I remembered that Grammy and I had had this, too, the ability to sit in a room, her sketching, me reading or playing solitaire on her computer, neither of us saying anything, but knowing the other was there. I'd always liked those afternoons of comfortable quiet, and it was really weird to find them again in this creepy house with Garrett McNamara and Olivia Willingham of all people.

Plus, painting was soothing, watching the pale greenish walls turn a warmer cream color. Looking at that, I was almost able to believe Live Oak House wasn't so scary after all. That the shadows and shapes, the weird thing in the attic, all of that was just a quirk of the house or something. Like having termites, only in this case the termites were ghosts.

Or something.

Garrett stepped back from the painting, holding one arm out and pointing his thumb up like the wall in front of him was some great work of art.

I laughed at him, and even Liv looked over and smiled.

"Dork," I said, and he sat down on the floor, smiling.

"You know, that color really makes this room seem less gross," he said. "Maybe people will actually have parties and weddings and things here after all."

I shrugged, swiping a stripe of paint across the plaster wall. "It would take a lot more than paint to make me party in here, but it doesn't hurt."

Garrett shrugged. "Nah, you could make it the whole theme of the wedding. Weddings have themes, right?"

Olivia laid down her own paintbrush, sitting on the floor, too, legs crossed. "What, 'A Very Ghostly Wedding' or something? 'Haunted Honeymoon'?"

"'Weird Wedding,'" Garrett and I said at almost the exact same time, and then we both laughed.

He shook his head. "This place really isn't all that weird, though, you know? Just old and full of crap."

I widened my eyes at that, and saw Liv make a similar face.

"I don't know," I said. "I definitely feel like some . . . things have gone on in here."

Liv and I hadn't told anyone about the attic or the music box, maybe because we didn't want anyone to make fun of us, or maybe because it felt like something we didn't want to get into.

Or maybe because it was ours.

"Like what?" he asked. "Spooky sounds, creepy dolls, lots of dead stuff?" He shrugged, his shoulders narrow underneath his bright pink T-shirt. "That's the house. Besides, if there were any ghosts, they'd totally go after those weird kids from Greene County, right?"

He suddenly rapped his knuckles on the floor, the sound too loud. "Hey, ghosts!" he called, and I instinctively moved forward, waving my hands and shushing him.

"Do you *want* to be eaten?" I asked. "Ghost-eaten?"

Then I felt dumb because he laughed and knocked on the floor again. "If you eat kids, ghosts, you want the Greene County kids, okay?"

Garrett was still laughing when he leaned back, putting both hands behind him to brace himself. And then his laugh turned into a yelp as he suddenly shot to his feet, one elbow catching the open paint can near him, sending Eggshell Sunlight oozing out across the hardwood. I don't think I'd ever seen anyone move that fast.

Well, I hadn't until Olivia shot to *her* feet as paint spread near the bottom of her sneaker. One second, the three of us had been joking, and the next, we were all standing up, staring at each other. My heart was pounding, and when I looked back at Garrett, for a second I thought there must have been another can of paint near us or something, a red one, because fat red drops were dripping from his palm, leaving bright stains on his white Vans.

And then I realized he was bleeding.

"Omigosh," I said in one big rush. "You cut yourself!"

Garrett looked back down at where he'd been sitting, frowning at the floor. "Y-yeah," he said unsteadily, his gaze still scanning the spot where he'd been. "I guess I did."

Olivia had already whipped one of the spare towels out of her equipment caddy and was handing it to him. "Is it bad?" she asked. "Should we go get Mrs. Freely?"

Garrett was a little pale, but he pressed the cloth to his palm and shook his head. "No, I don't think it's a big deal."

Olivia was crouched down near where Garrett had been sitting. "If it was a nail, you need a tetanus shot," she said, because if there was one thing Olivia could be counted on, it was to go worst-case scenario. "But I don't see anything," she went on, lightly running her hand over the floor. There were still some drops of blood on the dark wood, and she avoided those.

"It probably was a nail," I said. "What else could it be?"

I glanced over at Garrett and saw that he had moved the towel and was staring at his palm and then, I swear, he actually *swayed* on his feet.

I stepped forward to take his hand. "Boys," I muttered.

"It wasn't a nail," he said weakly, and I looked for myself at the wound just there at the meaty place on his palm at the base of his thumb.

And then I felt like *I* might start swaying.

Garrett was right. It wasn't a scrape on his hand, or a neat hole from a nail.

It was a *bite*.

CHAPTER 21

OLIVIA

"Can a house give you rabies?"

I twisted in the seat to scowl at Ruby. We were all headed home early that day because of Garrett. Mrs. Freely had taken him to the hospital to get his bite checked out, afraid there was a rabid raccoon or something loose in the house. It didn't matter how many times we told her we hadn't seen anything, that Garrett had been sitting in the middle of the room, so it wasn't like there was anywhere for an animal to hide, that we would've seen something if there had been. It couldn't have even been hiding under the floorboards because that room had a solid concrete floor. No, it had just been the three of us, the only people—things, whatever—in the room.

But then, it had to be an animal. Bites didn't *appear* out of nowhere.

"The house didn't bite him," I told Ruby now, keeping my voice low. Everyone was talking about Garrett, of course, wondering if there was some kind of wild animal loose in the house, and if there was, didn't that mean that we couldn't clean there anymore? That couldn't be safe. Maybe the rest of the summer would see us all singing "Kumbaya" in the rec center after all.

"Okay, but something did, and you and I both know it wasn't an animal," Ruby answered. The blue streak in her hair was tucked behind her ear, but she tugged at it now, pulling it in front of her eyes briefly before tucking it back into place. "It was something else, and I bet the hospital is gonna say so, too."

I squirmed in my seat, looking out the window, watching the town roll by. I still felt jumpy and weird, like the adrenaline hadn't worn off yet, plus blood always freaked me out. There hadn't been much on Garrett's hand, but there had been enough.

"He had *just* joked about the house eating people, and then he got bitten," Ruby said.

"So the house has *ears and teeth*?" I asked, wrinkling my nose, and Ruby mimicked my expression.

"I don't know," she admitted, then glanced behind her at the other kids. Susanna had apparently sneaked her phone into her pocket today, because she was keeping it low and clearly texting people. Wesley was staring out the window, and the other two boys were asleep again. I was beginning to wonder if there was something wrong with all of them.

"Do you want to come to my house?" Ruby said suddenly.

I looked over at her, feeling my eyebrows slide up to my bangs.

"Your house?" I repeated. Outside, the town was sliding past, a blur of green trees and bright flowers, red mailbox flags raised, and white shutters.

Ruby made a face at me. "Yeah, my house. My domicile. Mi casa. The place in which I abode."

My phone was wedged in my back pocket—I knew it was against the rules, but hey, what if there was an emergency?—and I squirmed on the seat to get it out. "Let me text my mom and ask if I can," I said, and I thought Ruby actually looked a little surprised. Had she thought I'd say no?

Well, I couldn't really blame her for that. *I* had thought I'd say no, to be honest. But today had been weird, and other than Garrett, there was no one but Ruby who knew about all that weird. It might be nice to talk it out rather than whispering in the van.

Mom's reply came in fast, a quick *Sure!* followed by, *Do you need me to come pick you up after?*

I asked Ruby, but she shook her head. "My mom can drive you back. She gets off work at four today. Or you can ride back on my bike. It's not that far."

I remembered that back when Emma and Ruby had been friends, Ruby had been around a lot, especially in the summer. She must have ridden her bike over, but I'd never really noticed. I didn't think she lived all that close, honestly, but then, Ruby's mom seemed a lot less strict than mine.

We stopped at the rec center, the van pulling into its usual space, and I slid across the seat, trying to keep my sweaty legs from making an embarrassing sound on the leather. Ruby's bike was locked up on the rack by the doors, and as we walked over to it, I noticed for the first time that it was a really nice bike. Bright green, thin tires, a line of multicolored beads on one spoke.

Ruby saw me looking and grinned. "The best, right? My grammy got it for me last year for Christmas."

That wasn't the first time Ruby had mentioned her grandmother. My own grandparents lived in Florida and California, and we didn't see them all that much, but Ruby's grandmother had lived here in town. I remembered her picking Ruby up from our house a few times. And then I remembered Ruby saying she'd hoped Emma might come back around to being her friend after her grandmother died, and I realized I didn't really know what to say to her about all this. So I smiled and nodded at the bike. "I like the beads."

Ruby turned back, briefly touching those beads with a finger before standing up, the bike lock on her hand, and gesturing for me to sit on the handlebars. "Come on," she said. "It's not far, and you can wear my helmet."

I stared at the helmet she offered me. It was black with a ridge of neon-yellow spikes coming out from the top, like a Mohawk or the back of a dinosaur or something. I wasn't sure how I'd never noticed Ruby in that thing before, but I took it and strapped it to my head, gingerly climbing onto the handlebars, the metal hot even though the bike had been parked in the shade.

"Ready?" Ruby asked, climbing onto the bike.

I held on tightly, reminding myself that if I could go to a possibly haunted house every day, riding a block on the handlebars of a bike should not be that scary.

"Ready," I said.

CHAPTER 22

RUBY

I have to hand it to Olivia—she only shrieked *once* on the ride to my house, which felt like a real victory for both of us.

Of course, I tried to be as careful as I could, and didn't even speed up coming over the bump at the top of my driveway, a major sacrifice since that's my favorite part of the bike ride home. Maybe that meant Liv and I really *were* becoming friends.

We both hopped off the bike at the garage door, and I went over and punched in the code to open it, walking my bike inside as Olivia followed behind me, unstrapping her—well, *my*—helmet.

"Do you want something to drink?" I asked, nodding at the older fridge we kept out there and leaning my bike against the wall.

"Sure," she said as she handed me the helmet, and I grabbed a couple of really cold sodas before we made our way into the house. "I get that we can't have Cokes at camp," I told Olivia, walking into the kitchen, "because sugar and caffeine or whatever, but don't you think that might actually help us work? I feel like I'd be so much more efficient all hopped up on Dr Pepper."

Liv laughed, taking a sip of her own drink. "I don't mind not having Cokes," she said, "but I wish they'd give us something better than those juice boxes. They're always warm and it's not sweet enough."

"Right? I hate that stuff. It's like drinking sweat."

"Oh, *gross*," Olivia immediately replied, fake-gagging, but then she laughed, like, *really* laughed and I started laughing, too. I don't think it was that my joke was that funny—definitely not my best work—but it felt good to giggle about something as stupid as bad lemonade after everything that had happened today. And I think maybe we were trying to avoid talking about Garrett and that bite and what it all might mean for as long as we could. But then eventually our giggles died down, and I cleared my throat, gesturing around.

"Do you want the tour? It takes like ten seconds."

She shrugged. "Sure."

I'd been to Olivia's house a bunch because of Emma, so I knew my house was really, really different. To be honest, I liked our place a lot better even though it was smaller. Emma and Olivia's house was pretty, all white cushions and blue curtains, lots of windows and plants, but it always looked like an advertisement for a furniture store or something. There was no *flair*, as Mom would've said.

Our house had plenty of flair. There was the one wall we'd sponge-painted with gold paint, the colorful pillows all over the couch, the furniture that didn't really match but still managed to go together. It was a little crazy and a lot cluttered, but it was ours, and I could tell Liv liked it. She smiled as she glanced around, and that honestly made me like her more than I'd thought I could.

"C'mon," I told her, "to my secret lair."

She went to set her soda on the counter, and I gave her a look. "Oh, no," I told her. "This is a total 'food and drink allowed in bedrooms' house. It's anarchy."

Giggling, Olivia toasted me with her can, then followed me through the den and the little hallway to my room.

It was messy in there, but I liked to think it was organized chaos. I swept a stack of books off the navy-blue beanbag chair I'd gotten at Target a few months back—saved up my own money, thank you very much—and gestured for her to sit on it while I perched on the edge of my futon. I used to have a much bigger, nicer bed, but I'd liked the idea of a bed that was also a couch. Sometimes I didn't even bother folding it out. I remembered that Liv's bed was this giant four-poster thing, all white and pink. Emma had made fun of it to me in secret, but I'd kind of liked it. It was pretty.

"Okay," I said once Olivia was sitting down. "Are we ready to talk about the bite thing?"

She took a deep breath, her fingers fiddling with the pop top on her soda can. "It was probably an animal," she offered, and I tucked my legs underneath me, giving her what I hoped was my best "girl, please" look.

"Olivia. Liv. Livtastic. Liv of my life."

She waved a hand, her cheeks a little pink. "I know, I know, the room was empty, we didn't see anything . . . I know all that stuff, Ruby, but . . . houses don't bite."

"This isn't a normal house," I reminded her. "Look, if *my* house took a chunk out of my palm—"

"It was barely a puncture."

"And left me with only half a hand, then sure, I'd be like, 'Animal, probs.' Who knows, there could be a rabid squirrel in that pile of laundry *right there*."

Olivia glanced over at the overflowing laundry basket I was pointing at, and scooted slightly away from it, pulling her legs closer.

"But this is Live Oak House," I went on. "A house with a history. And a house with a *tree* in the middle of it."

"But it's a *house*," Liv countered. "Made of wood and bricks and . . . I don't know, whatever they build houses of. It doesn't have *teeth*."

A house with teeth.

That's what I'd thought that first day when we'd driven up and I'd seen all those sharp angles and tall points. It had seemed stupid at the time, but it didn't seem all that stupid anymore.

I sat back on the futon, my heels clanging against the metal frame. "Then what bit Garrett?"

Liv leaned back, too, mimicking my posture as best she could on the beanbag chair. "We'll find out on Wednesday," Liv reminded me. "I'm sure the hospital can find out what kind of bite it was, and it was probably a raccoon or something. That . . . just moved really fast."

"We had a raccoon under our porch last year," I told her. "It moved about as fast as you'd expect something made of blubber and tiny hands to move."

"Raccoons don't have blubber," Olivia said, but I ignored that, pulling my satchel up onto my bed.

"And we don't have to wait for Wednesday, anyway," I told her. "I can text Garrett and ask him right now. He might already be back."

I fished my phone out of the backpack, then looked up to see Olivia staring at me, green eyes wide. "You have his *phone number*?" she nearly squeaked. "His actual phone number?"

Stupid as it was, I felt my face go hot. "Okay, it is not like that," I said, pulling up Garrett's contact info. "Like, at *all*. We were talking on Xbox Live the other day, and he gave it to me in case I ever needed to text him for . . . stuff. Xbox stuff, or school stuff. Not . . . not, like . . . other stuff."

Olivia didn't look all that convinced, and I thought about Emma again. Had Olivia said anything to her? Could I even ask if she had?

I busied myself sending Garrett the most casual text I possibly could. Once it was done, I hit send and looked up at Olivia. "Okay, done. Let's see what he says."

But Olivia was getting up off the beanbag chair to sit next to me on the futon, craning her neck to see the phone. "'Hey, Dude Man'?" she read, wrinkling her nose, and I pulled the phone back, tucking it under my leg.

"I was trying to be casual," I told her. "Friendly."

"You sound like an alien who just learned Earth-speak," Olivia replied, and I actually gaped at her. Like, mouth falling open, eyes wide, the whole thing.

"That was super rude," I informed her, "but also really funny? What is even happening right now?"

Rolling her eyes at me, Liv sat back on the futon, but she was smiling, too, and I wondered how often anyone had ever called her funny. Probably never, and I couldn't really blame them, since up until about six seconds ago, I certainly wouldn't have said that— My phone vibrated under my leg, and I snatched it up, wanting to see what Garrett had said. *Not* because of liking a boy reasons, but extremely serious haunted house reasons.

"'Weirdest thing,'" I read. "'Not an animal. Freely asked if one of you guys bit me lol.'"

Olivia and I looked up, meeting each other's eyes. "What?" she said softly, and I typed back my own version of that, an abbreviation that would've gotten me in trouble if Mom had seen it.

I waited for a while, holding my phone, occasionally glancing up at Liv to see her staring down at the phone screen, too. And then the answer flashed up, and both of us let out our breaths in a whoosh.

Because the bite was human.

CHAPTER 23

OLIVIA

"Well, I didn't bite him," Ruby said later as we sat in her room eating pizza. Her mom had come home earlier, and I'd gotten permission from *my* mom to stay for dinner. At my house, there is no way we would've been allowed to have dinner in my room, but Ruby's mom had smiled, called it a "carpet picnic," and left us alone. That was nice, since we really needed to talk in privacy.

"I obviously didn't bite him, either," I replied, picking a stray mushroom off my slice of pizza. "And there was no one in the room but the three of us."

Wrinkling her nose, Ruby leaned back against her futon, a slice of supreme pizza dangling from her hand in a way that made me nervous for the carpet. "You know, I think I'm more offended that Freely thought we might have bitten Garrett than I am scared that some ghost obviously bit Garrett."

"A ghost didn't bite him," I said automatically, because what else could I say? Nothing else really made sense, but when you had reached the point where "a ghost did it" seemed like the most logical explanation, things were pretty far gone in my opinion.

Ruby snorted, tugging at a string of cheese on her pizza. Her nails were painted dark blue with little sparkles, the polish chipped. "Then what did?" she asked, and since I didn't have an answer for that—and Ruby knew it—she just kept going.

"And this is the third creepy thing that's happened to us so far in there. It's only been two weeks, and we've got the music box, the key, and the attic. Which could've been some old music box malfunctioning, sure, and a key that *happened* to be lying in it. And the door could've been some trick of the architecture, or an open window making drafts do weird things. We can explain those things away if we want to, but Garrett having a *person bite* on his hand? How do we explain that away, Liv?"

I didn't bother telling her not to call me that—Ruby had clearly decided I needed a nickname whether I wanted one or not. I set my pizza on the paper plate, cleaning my hands off with a paper towel, and really tried to think. There was a poster of some video game over Ruby's bed, a tall dude in a hooded cloak holding daggers out to either side of him, and I focused on Dagger Guy as I thought.

"Maybe it's Garrett," I finally said. "Maybe it's some kind of elaborate prank. He seems like a little bit of a jerk—"

"Offense!" Ruby broke in, and I lowered my head, giving her a look.

"Ruby."

Sighing, Ruby scratched the back of her neck. "He is a little bit of a jerk," she agreed reluctantly. "But the *funny* kind. *I'm* the funny kind of jerk, Liv."

"No, you're not," I said, quicker than I meant to.

And when Ruby just stared at me, I drummed my fingers on my leg, not meeting her gaze. "You're funny, yes," I said, "but you're never mean. You're just . . . you."

There was a pause, and then Ruby said, "So you like my kind of jerkiness," and I shook my head even as I smiled.

"We're not talking about you, we're talking about Garrett," I said. "Is he the type of jerk who would somehow actually hurt himself to trick us into thinking he'd been bitten?"

We both pondered that for a second before, almost in unison, shaking our heads.

"That's major psychopath behavior," Ruby said, crossing her legs as she took another slice of pizza out of the box. "Garrett can be a jerk, but he's not evil or anything."

"Agreed," I said, then chewed on my thumbnail, thinking some more.

"So if it is a ghost . . . ," I started, and Ruby paused, her pizza halfway to her mouth, eyes wide.

"You're going to admit that we're dealing with the spooky?"

I waved her off and shoved my own plate away. "I'm just saying I'm open to the idea that something very weird is going on at Live Oak House, and it would be stupid not to explore all the options."

"All the options," Ruby echoed, nodding. "Especially now that people are getting hurt." Then she dropped her pizza on her plate with a *splat* and got to her feet, going over to the messy desk by her window. I'd spotted the desk when I'd first come in even though it was almost completely covered in books, paper, little plastic figurines of monsters, what looked to be an abandoned terrarium, and more colored pencils than I'd ever seen in one place before. To my eyes, it was all chaos, but Ruby went straight for what she was looking for, a thick black notebook covered in silver Sharpie doodles.

"We need to make a list," she said. "All the things that could possibly be going on at Live Oak House."

It was actually a pretty smart idea, and I scooted closer to her as she opened the notebook, flipping past several pages of drawings before finding a blank page. Then, at the top of that page, she scrawled THE SPOOKY in big purple letters.

"So, number one, obviously ghosts," she said, and I nodded, watching her write Ghosts, then draw a squiggly little figure next to it.

"Number two," Ruby went on, "we are being dumb."

I frowned at that, but then, after a moment, nodded. "Yeah, that's definitely one of the options."

Dumb went on the list, and Ruby made a quick sketch of two stick-figure-type girls, both holding their fingers up as big Ls on their foreheads.

"For losers," she informed me, and I turned my frown on her.

"Yeah, I got that."

The rest of the list went quickly, and was actually pretty short.

Ghosts.

Dumb.

Garrett. (His face drawn quickly, floppy hair over his brow, a smirk on his face.)

Invisible Monster. (No drawing for that one, of course.)

Mrs. Freely. (I didn't want to add that one, but Ruby insisted that we at least consider it an option.)

The two of us looked at the list for a moment, Ruby tapping the pen against the paper, a sound that would have annoyed me once.

"Anything else?" she asked at last, and I shook my head.

"Nothing I can think of."

Ruby added ?????? at the very bottom, then gave me a shrug. "Covering all our bases," she told me.

So we had a handful of weird experiences and now we had a list of things that might be causing them, but I wasn't sure what we should do next. I asked Ruby, and she leaned against her bed, thinking.

"It pains me to say this," she said on a sigh, "but I think we might have to do, like, schoolwork. Research. The library. Stuff like that. And don't get me wrong, that's totally against everything I stand for in the summer, but if we want to get to the bottom of this, it seems like the only way."

I gave a sort of giggling-snorting laugh, the kind that always embarrassed me but I was never able to help, and Ruby looked at me, her eyes crinkling in the corners.

"What was *that*?"

"That was me laughing," I told her, "and I'm laughing because . . . 'get to the bottom of this.' It's like we're in a Scooby-Doo mystery or something."

Ruby laughed, too, tilting her head back against the futon, and then she picked up her list and added *Old Man Jenkins* at the bottom.

We were still giggling when her mom came upstairs to tell us it was time for me to head home.

RubyToozday: Sooooo JACKPOT. I went to the library today, and they had the book about Live Oak House.

OliviaAnneWillingham: Anything good?

RubyToozday: YES. Check this out:

RubyToozday: "Live Oak House was built in 1903 by Felix Wrexhall, a man fleeing a tragic past."

RubyToozday: I mean, BOOM, TRAGIC PAST RIGHT OFF THE BAT.

OliviaAnneWillingham: What kind of "tragic past"?

RubyToozday: I'll get to that. Then there's THIS: "However, from the very first day construction on his new dream home began, it seemed like the house was cursed."

OliviaAnneWillingham: Ooooh!

RubyToozday: I KNOW RIGHT.

RubyToozday: Okay, now I'm going to summarize.

RubyToozday: Felix wanted the very first thing put in the house to be . . . wait for it . . . the live oak tree.

RubyToozday: You're shocked, I know.

RubyToozday: He wanted to have it installed in the foundation of the house as this massive pillar right there when you walked in, rising up from the floor all the way to the third story.

RubyToozday: And that part worked out, we see it every day, it looks cool, etc.

RubyToozday: But the NOT-COOL PART?

RubyToozday: It killed someone.

OliviaAnneWillingham: Seriously?

RubyToozday: Like I'd joke about Murder Trees. YES.

RubyToozday: So the tree had to travel by rail, and three different men working for the railroad company had been injured loading it up for the journey. One had his leg crushed when the trunk unexpectedly rolled off the flatbed car it was riding on. Another was nearly killed when the machinery moving the tree misfired, sending it swinging right at the guy's head. A third lost a hand getting the trunk off the train and onto the stretcher they'd set up to literally drag the tree out to where the house was being built.

RubyToozday: Oh, and a horse dropped dead dragging it out there, but I wasn't going to mention that part because it's sad. :(

RubyToozday: The point is, by the time that special tree got to the site where Live Oak would be built, it had already done some damage, and it was about to do a lot more.

OliviaAnneWillingham: Do we think the tree is why the house went creepy? Are we dealing with an evil tree here?

RubyToozday: Maybe? We can look into any cases of evil trees, I guess.

RubyToozday: That will be a fun search history to explain to my mom.

RubyToozday: Anyway, the tree finally made it to the building site. At that point, they'd laid a foundation and everything, but Felix was really serious about the live oak being the first "real" piece of the house put in place. That day—May 4, 1903—was supposedly really nice. Bright blue sky, a little bit of breeze rustling through the leaves, everyone decked out in their Sunday best. People from Chester's Gap came to watch, and Felix had even hired a little band to play music while they all watched the tree get put in place.

RubyToozday: This story is really making me realize how awful things were before television. Can you imagine? "Get in the wagon, kids, we're going to watch someone PUT A TREE IN A HOUSE."

OliviaAnneWillingham: Our town isn't that much more interesting now, I have to say.

RubyToozday: Truth.

OliviaAnneWillingham: Also, are you typing this from the book, or are you still putting it in your own words?

RubyToozday: This is all me. That's why it sounds dumb.

OliviaAnneWillingham: It doesn't! That's why I was wondering.

OliviaAnneWillingham: It actually sounds really good. You should totally turn this whole thing into a book one day.

RubyToozday: STAHP.

RubyToozday: Okay, so, the big day. Band playing, perfect weather, people wearing a lot of white, probably some cool hats. The men go to place the tree. It was lifted up by some kind of early crane type deal with ropes and pulleys, and then there were a bunch of guys at the bottom, ready to set the trunk in place. Everyone was watching, and it seemed to be going well until suddenly and without any warning, the chains holding the tree snapped.

RubyToozday: Crashed to the ground there in front of everyone.

RubyToozday: ON everyone, basically.

RubyToozday: Okay, only on two people, thankfully. Everybody scattered as it started to fall, but one of the workmen and Felix Wrexhall weren't so lucky.

RubyToozday: I mean, the workman was the unluckiest of all— he died.

RubyToozday: Felix only got his leg crushed, and was NOT squashed. BUT! Live Oak House had claimed its first victim.

OliviaAnneWillingham: Its only, right? No one else has died WEIRDLY in that house.

OliviaAnneWillingham: No one has even lived in it except Felix, his wife, and his son, and they all died of old age.

RubyToozday: TRUE. But the point is, from that very first day, people started talking about Live Oak House and wondering if there was something wrong with it. If it was cursed in some way.

OliviaAnneWillingham: I feel like Killer Tree Cursed.

RubyToozday: Right, but people still thought it was an accident. It was an accident. It's not like anyone dropped a tree on Felix on purpose.

RubyToozday: OR DID THEY?

OliviaAnneWillingham: So what was his tragic past?

RubyToozday: Oh, right, that. It's all mysterious, and no one would talk about it, but basically, Felix Wrexhall just shows up here in Chester's Gap after buying some lumber factory. He came from somewhere in Georgia with his wife, Lucy, and his family had been killed in a fire or something.

OliviaAnneWillingham: But what about Lucy's family? The twins?

RubyToozday: There's nothing about Lucy. Seriously, it's like she just started EXISTING when she moved here. Was already married to Felix, they had a baby, and Garrett said she eventually went to some hospital because she'd kind of lost it.

RubyToozday: Her mind, that is, not the baby.

RubyToozday: Her baby was Mr. Matthew.

RubyToozday: ANYWAY!

RubyToozday: And the tree—like, THE TREE—is from his family's old farm.

RubyToozday: But here's my thing: The house has been around for over a hundred years. One person dies, no one else, and there are creepy stories, but nothing like what we've been seeing.

RubyToozday: So why this summer?

RubyToozday: That house has been there for literally a thousand summers.

OliviaAnneWillingham: No, it has not.

RubyToozday: Literally a thousand. And suddenly, THIS summer, Mrs. Freely is all, "Oh, yeah, let me send some kids in to clean this super creepy house! And feed it their blood!"

OliviaAnneWillingham: One kid cutting his hand is not feeding the house blood, Ruby.

RubyToozday: I SAW A MOVIE LIKE THAT ONCE, THOUGH.

RubyToozday: Where to keep the town, like, successful and crops growing or something, all the grown-ups were feeding the occasional kid to some kind of corn monster.

RubyToozday: (I was not supposed to watch that movie, probably.)

OliviaAnneWillingham: I'm not saying there aren't weird things going on at the house.

OliviaAnneWillingham: There are. I'm just not sure they're THAT weird.

RubyToozday: Do you have any other idea what might be going on?

OliviaAnneWillingham: No, I don't.

OliviaAnneWillingham: But I need more than "I saw this in a movie once" to think that Mrs. Freely is behind all the creepy stuff.

RubyToozday: She was related to the Wrexhalls, though, remember?

RubyToozday: A distant cousin or something, not close enough to inherit, but still PART OF THE FAMILY.

RubyToozday: I wonder if there's anything in her office.

RubyToozday: Like some history about the house.

RubyToozday: Or a contract signed in blood, promising to give the house the souls of bad kids.

OliviaAnneWillingham: Oh, yeah, I bet she keeps that right next to her package of highlighters. Probably on top of sheet music for "Kumbaya."

RubyToozday: We've talked about you being funny . . .

RubyToozday: It's unsettling and not okay, please stop.

RubyToozday: Maybe we won't find something that obvious, but there could be something. At least a hint that Mrs. Freely knew all the creepy stories but sent us in anyway.

OliviaAnneWillingham: She had to have known them. Garrett had heard stories, and you said you'd heard a few things, too. It seems like the town council would at least be AWARE, right?

RubyToozday: You'd think.

RubyToozday: So we're agreed that we need to break into Mrs. Freely's desk.

OliviaAnneWillingham: Um, no.

OliviaAnneWillingham: We are so very NOT in agreement on that.

RubyToozday: And we'll do it on Monday, good plan.

OliviaAnneWillingham: Ruby.

OliviaAnneWillingham: RUBY.

CHAPTER 24

RUBY

"Do you believe in ghosts?" I asked Mom as I closed the chat window with Liv.

Only a few seconds before, Mom had been moving around my room, picking up things, hanging my clothes on hangers, doing her typical "Mom in my room" thing, but now she stopped and looked at me. That was never a good sign with Mom. Running her own business meant that Mom was an A-plus multitasker, so if she actually stopped doing three things at once to listen to me, it meant she was taking this seriously, and I wasn't sure I wanted that.

And I *definitely* didn't want it when she tilted her head down a little, the bright pink stripe of hair she usually had tucked behind one ear sliding forward to curl around her jaw. "Is this about Grammy?" she asked, and yeah, definitely regretted bringing that up.

"No," I said quickly, closing the book on Live Oak House and moving over to sit on my bed. But it was too late. Mom was looking around again, her eyes settling on the stack of library books by my bed with all their *GHOSTS!* and *HAUNTINGS* titles.

She frowned then, dimples showing up in her cheeks. My face did that same thing, dimples showing up not when I smiled, but when I scowled.

"Rubes," Mom said, sitting on the edge of the bed. "We can talk about this if you want to."

"It's not about Grammy," I told her, then bit my lower lip hard enough that it hurt a little bit. "I wouldn't want Grammy to be a ghost."

To my surprise, Mom smiled at that. "She'd be so bad at it," she said with a little laugh, and suddenly I wanted to laugh and cry at the same time. Mom leaned over, wrapping an arm around my shoulders. "Stealing all our Girl Scout cookies," Mom went on. "Bumping into doors because she wouldn't wear her glasses."

Now the laughing feeling was stronger than the crying one, and I leaned into Mom's hug. "Putting records on in the middle of the night," I added, and Mom nodded.

"Linda Ronstadt," she said. "Maybe Emmylou."

I smiled at that, remembering the way Grammy used to play music while she cooked dinner, singing along, dancing. She used to dance with me, too, and for once the memory didn't make me sad. It was a good one.

Her arm still around me, Mom asked, "So what *are* the ghost books about, then?"

For a second, I thought about telling her about the house, the weird things that were going on.

But then I thought she might talk to Mrs. Freely, or make

me not go back, and I felt like I was onto something there. Plus, it was kind of fun, hunting ghosts with Olivia. Whoever would have thought Olivia could be *fun*?

So I shrugged and said, "Curious, I guess. There are like a million shows on ghosts, and you're always saying you want me to find some hobbies."

Mom raised her eyebrows, the little silver ball in the left one flashing. "So you want to start hunting ghosts as a hobby?"

Even after what I'd experienced at Live Oak House, I wasn't really into the idea of *that*. One Hall of Heads was bad enough, but seeking out more of them on purpose? No, thanks.

Still, I sat up on my bed and lifted one shoulder, like I was thinking it over. "Not sure yet," I said. "But keeping a lot of options open."

Shaking her head, Mom stood and picked up the nearest book, a green one called *Am I Haunted?* On the front, a guy with spiky black hair stared out at the camera while really bad Photoshopped spirits twined around his outstretched arms. "I think I've been on a date with this guy," she mused, and I laughed, taking the book from her.

"You've definitely been on a date with a guy with hair this bad," I teased, and she gave an exaggerated grimace.

Watching me slide the book back into its stack, Mom folded her arms over her chest. The V wasn't there between her eyebrows anymore, so I figured we were okay. Or getting there.

"Promise to tell me if any of that reading gets too heavy or scary, right?" she asked, and I gave a quick nod.

"Absolutely. And if I don't, the fact that I'm sleeping on your floor should be a dead giveaway."

Mom snorted at that, closing her eyes and shaking her head again. "You're a mess, Ruby," she told me, and I lifted my hands, palms up.

"Learned from the best."

This was an old routine of ours, one I think Mom used to do with Grammy, and one I'd always liked. We were messes, both of us, really. Grammy probably had been, too. But we loved each other, and I thought that was probably more important than any of that other stuff, stuff like what Olivia and Emma Willingham had. I wouldn't trade my mom for theirs, even with pancake breakfasts every Saturday.

"Everything going good with Camp Chrysalis?" Mom asked, and I nodded.

"I'm learning many fun and unique ways to list things," I told her. "All sorts of lessons about old books and dead birds."

Mom had already moved to the door, and now she leaned against the jamb, arms folded. "Not exactly the best way to spend a summer, huh?"

It was maybe the worst way to spend a summer other than being packed off to some camp where singing and Chubby Bunny contests were on the menu every night, but I made myself look unconcerned.

"It's actually not so bad," I said, picking at a loose thread on my quilt. "Kind of boring, but the house is neat, and I have people to talk to."

I could feel my face going red at that, and hoped that I wasn't blushing, but moms are superheroes when it comes to figuring out stuff you don't want to talk about. "Are you talking to a booooooooyyyyyy?" she asked, her voice sliding up all those vowels, and if rolling my eyes were not a capital offense in our house, I so would've done it.

"There are boys there, yes, and sometimes I have to work with them, but I'm not *specifically* talking to boys."

Mom was still smiling at me. "Worse places to get a crush than over a bucket of disinfectant, I guess."

Lying down on my stomach, I kicked my feet in the air. "We actually don't clean anything," I told her. "Because Mrs. Freely doesn't want us breathing in chemicals."

"Oh, man," Mom said, snapping her fingers. "And here I was so looking forward to suing when you grew an extra head."

I giggled at that. "Sorry."

Giving an exaggerated sigh, Mom flopped down on the edge of my bed. "We'll find some other way to get that condo in Florida, I guess."

I nudged her with my elbow, and she kept smiling, but I noticed her eyes straying to the books again.

"It's nothing," I promised her again, but Mom was smarter than that.

"Is it the house?" she asked. "It looks pretty solid from the outside, but I can see where being in there every day might give anybody the heebie-jeebies."

Sitting up, I ran my fingers over the cover of *Am I Haunted?* "It's definitely a weird place," I told Mom, wondering how I could even describe Live Oak House. It wasn't that it was weird or old or creepy. It wasn't even that it felt all that haunted, really.

It was more like it felt . . . aware. Like someone was watching us all the time, waiting for us to put the pieces together.

"Did you ever get a bad feeling about a place?" I asked. "Like, you walked in somewhere, and it just felt . . . wrong? And if someone asked you, 'Hey, what's your problem with that place?' you wouldn't be able to say, really?"

By the end of that little spiel, Mom was frowning at me, and she reached out to tuck my hair behind my ear.

"Is that how Live Oak House is making you feel?" she asked, and I mulled over exactly how to answer that. I mean, of course it was, that's why we were talking about this and she knew it, but I still didn't want to come right out and say it. I didn't know if that was because saying it would make it feel real, or because I was worried that if I did, Mom would make me quit going there or would talk to Mrs. Freely.

In the end, I decided to come clean. "Yeah, but I don't want to stop going there."

I could tell that was a surprise, and Mom sat back slightly, tucking her chin into her neck. "Okaaaaay," she said slowly, and I sat up.

"It's a totally weird, creepy place with a totally weird, creepy feel," I told her, "but, like . . . it's fun? And definitely better than helping the teachers up at school scrape gum from under their desks or whatever else we could be doing. And as bizarre as this is going to sound, I've sort of started being friends with Olivia Willingham, and I feel like it's because of the house? I don't know, it's all really weird. Not the house—me and Liv being friends. Well, the house, too, that's weird and also a part of it, and I'm talking too much again, aren't I?"

Mom held up her thumb and forefinger, pinching them together. "Little bit," she confirmed, but she was smiling at me in that way she did sometimes, where her eyes looked warm and there were extra crinkles in the corners.

"But," Mom went on, "what I think you're *trying* to say is that you're having fun this summer after all, and even though things are weird at Live Oak House, you've made a friend."

"Made a friend *because* things are weird at Live Oak House," I clarified, and Mom nodded.

"Even so. And you don't want me storming up there, telling Mrs. Freely the house makes you creeped out, because that might mess up this fun thing you have going. Even though the fun thing also scares you a little bit."

I made finger-guns at her. "Nailed it."

Laughing, Mom shook her head, then leaned over to ruffle my hair. "You are the strangest child in the entire world, but you're my strange child, and I love you. And I will let you keep feeling weird in that house with your new friend in peace."

Relieved, I tilted forward so that I could hug her quickly. "Thanks, Mom."

She squeezed me back before getting off the bed and adding, "Just don't get eaten by a ghost and make me regret this, okay?"

"Deal."

CHAPTER 25

OLIVIA

I pretty much spent that entire Monday freaking out. Not because of the house—nothing actually happened that day, and cleaning was the good kind of boring—it was the idea of sneaking into Mrs. Freely's office that had my stomach in knots.

And looking at Ruby that morning, it was clear she was still planning on doing it. She spent most of the day giving me significant looks and at one point did some kind of pointing gesture that looked like she might be describing a complicated baseball play.

It wasn't that I didn't want to know what was going on at the house, but I wasn't sure there even *was* anything in Mrs. Freely's office, and if we got caught . . .

Mrs. Freely had *said* there would be consequences for misbehaving at Camp Chrysalis. I didn't bring that up to Ruby because she'd been there and heard it herself, and I didn't want to feel like I was . . . I don't know, nagging her or whatever. We'd gotten to be friends this summer, or at least close to it, and the last thing I wanted was for Ruby to roll her eyes at me or do that impatient sighing thing Em sometimes did. Ruby didn't say anything to me in the van on the way back to the rec center, and I was almost thinking she'd forgotten the whole plan when we sat down with our Responsibility Journals.

I'd just started my second paragraph (a total ramble about how I needed to be more responsible at home, even though that wasn't really true; I did plenty of work at home) when Ruby slid over from her place on the mat.

"This is the best chance we're going to get," she whispered. She was crouched next to me on the mat, almost in a runner's stance, like at any moment she was going to dash off. I looked at the toe of her sneaker and the bright red diamond shape she'd doodled on the white canvas part. A ruby, duh.

"Liv. Why are you staring at my shoe?"

I raised my eyes to Ruby's, not wanting to admit that I was stalling. "I don't think this is a good time," I told her, scooting over and looking around.

It's true that Mrs. Freely was nowhere in sight, but Lee and Leigh were over by the doors, talking to each other, and while Susanna and Wesley were writing in their journals, Garrett and those other two boys were sitting in a circle, talking and laughing in low voices.

Ruby followed my gaze. "They're not going to tell on us," she said with her usual Ruby Certainty. "Honor among thieves and all that."

I whipped my head back around. "I'm not a thief!"

Raising both hands, Ruby widened her eyes at me. "Whoa whoa whoa, relax. I know that. Just a figure of speech. Anyway, let's go while Lee and Leigh are still flirting."

They *were* flirting, I realized now. Leigh kept playing with her hair, and Lee was laughing too much.

Taking a deep breath, I put my journal down on the mat. "Okay," I told her. "Let's go."

Susanna glanced up at us as we rose to our feet, and I saw her exchange a look with Ruby before giving a slight nod and turning back to her journal.

"What was that about?" I asked as we ambled over in the direction of Mrs. Freely's office as casually as we could. If anyone saw us before we got inside, we could say we were going to the bathroom. It was in the same general direction as the office.

"Susanna said she'd keep an eye out just in case," Ruby told me, glancing back over her shoulder. Still no Mrs. Freely, and the boys were still talking, Lee and Leigh still too interested in each other to watch us.

"So Susanna knows we're breaking into the office?"

We'd reached the door by now, and Ruby shot me a look. "We're not breaking in, Liv, come on."

As though to prove her point, she pushed on the half-open door to Mrs. Freely's office and slipped inside.

For the space of a few seconds, I hesitated. I hadn't actually done the thing that got me sentenced to Camp Chrysalis, but this? This was the real deal. It might not be breaking in, exactly, but it was definitely sneaking and therefore definitely Not Okay.

But I thought again about Live Oak House, about Garrett's bite, the shape in the attic, the way the house itself seemed to be watching us wherever we were. Was it possible that Mrs. Freely knew something about this? And if she did, didn't we deserve to find out?

So I took a deep breath and followed Ruby inside.

The overhead fluorescent light was on, which actually made this whole thing feel less sneaky, something Ruby apparently noticed, too. "We should be in here at night, dressed all in black with flashlights," she whispered, and I frowned at her as she made her way over to the desk.

"That really would be breaking and entering, since we wouldn't be able to get into the rec center at night," I reminded her, and Ruby did that finger-guns thing at me.

"That's my Liv, always thinking. Okay, so file cabinet for me, desk for you?"

Chewing my lower lip, I looked between those two things, then shook my head. "No, reverse it. The file cabinet feels . . ."

"Less personal," Ruby finished, but she didn't tease me about it or remind me that whichever one I picked, it was still sneaking. She just nodded and made her way to the desk.

I tiptoed over to the file cabinet, not really sure why I was making such an effort to be quiet. Lee and Leigh were on the other side of the gym from the office, and I felt like Ruby was right in thinking the other kids wouldn't tell on us. Honor among thieves and all that.

Pulling the top drawer out as quietly as I could, I peered inside.

There was a row of brightly colored folders, all of which had a white sticker label on the top, our names scrawled across each one. Definitely not what we were looking for, but I had to admit, I was tempted to pull out my file and see what was written there. It was probably the paperwork our parents had to sign before we started.

Closing that drawer, I moved on to the second one.

More files.

Ruby was rifling through the top drawer of the desk, pulling out a pack of highlighters and a stack of Post-its. "There has to be something," she muttered, and I closed my drawer, turning to face her.

"Ruby, this is dumb," I said. "There's not going to be any-thing—"

But before I could finish, the door swung open and Mrs. Freely stood there. Her mouth opened and closed a few times, but no words came out, and I thought of how we must look, me with my back to the file cabinet, Ruby still holding on to the desk drawer.

"What on *earth* is going on in here?"

CHAPTER 26
RUBY

Mrs. Freely's office smelled like overly sweet fruit. Not a fruit I could even place, really, just Generic Gross Fruit Smell pumping out from one of the three air fresheners plugged in around the room.

I couldn't blame her for all the air fresheners—I'd use them, too, if I had to have boys in my office all the time.

Her chairs were light pink and green, the material scratchy under my legs, and I fought the urge to fidget, especially as Mrs. Freely gave us her best Serious Face from across the desk. It was actually nice to see that face instead of her usual grin.

I was used to *this* expression from grown-ups.

I didn't think Olivia was, though. She seemed to be shrinking into her chair, like she could camouflage herself. And honestly, she wears enough pastels that she probably could.

"Would the two of you like to tell me what you were doing in my office during Journal Time?" she asked, and I glanced over at Liv again, wondering if she'd go along with the fib I was working on.

"We were looking through your stuff for information about the house," Liv blurted out, and okay, so we weren't gonna go with fibbing, apparently.

But that didn't mean I couldn't turn this around with a little thing I liked to call the How Dare You! Defense. This is a move where, when *you've* done something wrong, you act like the person who caught you was in the wrong. It's bold and can sometimes go badly, but in this case, I thought it was worth a shot.

"It's not like we don't know what you're doing at Live Oak House," I said to Mrs. Freely, sitting up straight in my chair, pushing my shoulders back. "We were looking for proof."

Mrs. Freely's stern look gave way to something like confusion.

Real confusion, too.

Uh-oh.

"What I'm doing at Live Oak House? Other than trying to get it straightened up and letting you kids play a valuable part in bringing something beautiful to our community?"

Uggghhhh, that was a really good answer, and one that I didn't know how to reply to, really.

Luckily, Olivia had no problems with that. "No, we know that," she said, "and we really appreciate it. It's just that the house is . . ."

Mrs. Freely folded her hands on top of her desk and leaned forward. "The house is what?"

"It's super freaking creepy and haunted, and we're not going to let you feed us to it!" I said, and Olivia turned her head to look at me with wide eyes.

Seriously? she mouthed, but hey, we needed to get this all out in the open, and now that we were busted, it felt like the right time to call some bluffs.

"You knew there was something wrong with the house, and you put us all in there anyway," I went on, ignoring how both Mrs. Freely and Olivia were staring at me like I'd lost my mind.

"And why now? That house has been shut up forever, but all of a sudden, this summer, 'Ooooh, let's let the bad kids inside a house that *bites people.*'"

"Ruby," Mrs. Freely said, her voice sharp and strong. "First of all, the house does not bite, that's . . ." She shook her head, blinking, like that was such a bizarre idea, she didn't even know where to start. "And secondly, you're not 'bad kids.'"

"Of course we are," I argued, flopping back in my chair. "Why else would we be here at Camp Chrysalis? It's Bad Kid Camp, everyone knows that."

And then something really, really awful happened.

Mrs. Freely looked . . . sad. Like, the corners of her mouth turned down, and something went soft in her eyes, and I could see her fingers fluttering, clenching and unclenching.

I had made a grown-up sad.

Even if she was a grown-up who wanted to feed us to an evil house, that didn't feel good, and when I looked over at Olivia again and saw that she was scowling at me, the slithery feeling in my stomach got even worse.

"I've never thought of this as 'Bad Kid Camp,'" Mrs. Freely said at last. "I've thought of it as a place where kids who might have some trouble fitting in could feel like they were useful. Could make new friends, much like you and Olivia have done."

She gestured to Liv, who'd gone back to trying to sink into her chair. "Correct me if I'm wrong, but when we started the summer, I don't think you two were all that close, and now every day, I see you with your heads together, sitting next to each other in the van. Haven't you become friends?"

I opened my mouth to say that sure, we had, but that didn't take away from the "house eating us" thing, but then Liv said, "No, we're not. We were working together on finding out what was going on with the house, but that was stupid. We were stupid. And we're sorry we went through your stuff, Mrs. Freely, we really are. It won't happen again."

With that, she got up and nearly ran from the office, leaving Mrs. Freely and me to stare after her. That feeling in my stomach was worse now, and I muttered my own apology to Mrs. Freely before running out after Olivia.

I found her on the sidewalk outside the double doors, her arms across her chest.

"So we're not friends?" I said, because I think being direct is always the best plan, and my feelings were hurt. More hurt than I would've thought they could've been when it came to Olivia Willingham.

To my surprise, Liv rounded on me, her eyes bright. "No," she said. "You never really wanted to be my friend, anyway. You just wanted someone to go along with you on this . . . this . . ." After a second, she shook her head. "I don't even know why I'm here."

"Like, why you're with me, or why you're at Camp Chrysalis?" I asked, and I could feel my face getting hotter, like that hollow feeling in my stomach was clawing its way up my neck. "Because I don't know why you're here with me, hanging out and getting yogurt and stuff, if I'm apparently some user who was pulling you down for my own schemes or whatever it is that you think."

Olivia was watching me with her lips clamped shut, her arms still crossed, but I thought she flinched a little. Maybe that meant I was getting to her, and I was glad.

And maybe that's why I wanted to make her flinch even harder, and said, "And you're at Camp Chrysalis because your sister used you to get out of being in trouble. Just like she always said she would."

It was too far. I knew it the second the words left my lips, and I had never wanted to call anything back as badly as I did that last sentence. But it was too late, the words out now, every bit as sharp as I could have wanted them to be.

Liv wasn't like me. She didn't get angry like that, she just got *hurt*, and there was plenty of that in her big green eyes as she stared at me.

"What?" she nearly whispered, and I shook my head, mad at myself now.

"Nothing. I was just being a jerk."

And I was, but Liv was too smart—or knew me too well now—to just let it go. "She said that to you before, didn't she." It wasn't a question, and if my words had shot out, barbed and stinging like a dart, Liv's just fell from her mouth, flat and sad. "She said that she was going to do something and blame it on me."

"Not exactly," I said, moving a little closer to her, my hand flailing out like it wanted to pat her or hug her, but instead, just sort of waved near her. "She didn't say, 'Hey, I'm gonna shoplift some lipstick and blame Olivia!'" And she hadn't. I could say that with confidence.

"So what did she say?" Liv asked, turning wounded eyes to me, and ugh, for someone who could be so good at the occasional white lie, this one just didn't want to come out.

"Just that . . . I mean, she was joking, she was *totally* joking, but she had said before that one of the good things about having a twin was that there was always someone who looked just like you to blame things on if you had to."

I said the words really fast, like they were a Band-Aid I was ripping off, but they hurt anyway. I could see it in the way Liv held her elbows tighter and seemed to do that shrinking thing again.

"She didn't ask me to do it," Liv replied, and lifted her hand to tug a strand of hair off her sweaty cheek. "So it wasn't her fault, anyway—it was mine for saying something."

"Yes!" I nearly shouted, relieved. Then I thought for a second. "Well, no, it wasn't your fault, it was just . . . you know, all mixed up and stuff. It was one of those things that happen sometimes."

That was the dorkiest thing I'd ever said, and if anyone ever gave me the old "these things happen!" spiel, I might have punched them. But Liv just nodded and turned her head, looking down the drive for her mom's car.

I stood there, my hands hanging at my sides, waiting for the right thing to say to suddenly spring to my lips. There had to be something, right? Some magic words that would fix whatever it was that had just gone wrong between me and Liv?

But there was nothing. We just stood there in silence until Liv's mom's car came rolling up the drive, and when Liv climbed in the passenger seat, she didn't even look at me.

CHAPTER 27

OLIVIA

Chester's Gap was famous for its Christmas parade, but the town also did one for the Fourth of July. It wasn't nearly as big as the one they held during the holidays (or as fun to watch—last year, our Christmas parade had had little teacup Pomeranians riding on llamas, and that was hard to beat), but it was fun, and it was our family tradition to go eat at the Italian place at the edge of downtown before walking down to Main Street to watch the parade.

It was hot, of course, like it was every year, but this summer seemed especially brutal as we made our way from the restaurant to the parade route.

"Ugh, why do we always do Italian?" Mom wondered, moving her purse from one shoulder to the other.

"Tradition," replied Dad, and Mom shot him a look.

"But one we made up, right? One we could change? Maybe trade out for . . . I don't know, something lighter before we slog through nine thousand percent humidity."

Dad laughed, reaching out to take her hand, swinging their arms together in a way that was both embarrassing and also kind of sweet. "We'll hold a family meeting about it when Emma gets back."

He glanced over his shoulder at me. "What do you think, Livvy? Italian or something new?"

I shrugged, and I saw my parents catch each other's eye.

"Are you okay, honey?" Mom asked for what was probably the hundredth time in the past few days.

We had the week off from Camp Chrysalis for the Fourth, and to my surprise, Mrs. Freely hadn't called Mom about what had happened in her office.

I'd spent a few days waiting for the call, and when it hadn't come, I'd stopped feeling worried and started feeling . . . sad. About all of it, really: Ruby, getting in trouble, that thing she'd said about Emma.

That's why I'd been ignoring all of Em's calls, not sure what to say to her. "Did you do it on purpose?" was the only thing I wanted to know, but at the same time, I almost *didn't* want to know. What if she had? What would that mean?

Now I made myself smile at Mom, and said, "Too full to think about any food, I guess."

I wasn't sure if she believed that, but she dropped Dad's hand to take my shoulder, pulling me in between them. "This is weird, isn't it?" Mom asked. "Just the three of us, going to the parade." Then she gave me a little squeeze. "But nice."

I made myself smile at her. "Totally."

We found the spot we usually liked on the parade route, right down from Books on Main, near the fountain. There was a thick stretch of grass there, and the nice kind of grass, the expensive type that felt soft and didn't make the backs of your legs itch.

I sat down there and pulled my phone out of my pocket.

I'd promised Em that I'd put her on Hangouts when the parade was going so she didn't have to miss it, but it would be the first time we'd talked since the fight with Ruby.

I pressed her contact and waited for her to pick up, wondering if she'd be alone in her cabin this time or if there would be another girl there, wanting to see the parade with her.

Maybe her whole cabin.

In a weird way, I kind of hoped that would happen, because then it would mean I *couldn't* ask her about the lipstick thing.

But when she answered, there was just her, her face sort of shadowed.

"Has it started?" she asked, and I turned my phone so she could see.

"Not yet."

I pointed the phone at Mom and Dad, both of whom were sitting a little closer to the curb than I was. "Say hi," I instructed, and they both waved at Emma, who waved back, calling out, "Hiiiii!"

When I turned the phone back to me, Emma looked . . . well, it was hard to tell, really. It was still dim on her end of the phone, but she blinked a few times, and there wasn't the same excitement and . . . Emma-ness, I guess, that I'd been expecting.

"Where are you?" I asked, just as the drums started up somewhere down the parade line.

"In my bunk," she said, and now that she'd said it, I could

make out the purple of her blanket, the one Mom had bought her for camp.

"Are you by yourself?" I asked, and she nodded.

"Everyone is at the campfire, but I didn't want to miss the parade."

And then she sighed. "I wish I was there with y'all to see it in person, though."

I glanced up at Mom and Dad. They were both craning their necks to look down the parade route, and, I thought, very deliberately trying *not* to listen to me and Em.

It was sweet, but I still stood up and pointed back toward the parking lot. "I'll be over here for a sec," I told them, even as Emma said, "Wait, what?"

"Why?" Dad asked, but Mom touched his arm and they exchanged a look. I'd never realized that my parents could do the whole silent-communication thing me and Em had perfected, but they clearly could, because Dad finally nodded and said, "Don't go far, and make sure you can see us."

"Got it!" I replied, and then jogged far enough away that they couldn't overhear me.

Emma was frowning at the screen. "The point of this was to *see* the parade, Livvy," she said.

"Are you homesick?" I asked, scratching my ankle with the tip of my shoe. "Or is camp not fun anymore or something?"

Em wrinkled her nose. "It's okay, I guess? But I am getting *so tired* of archery and canoeing, and Sasha was being *totally* rude to me at lunch—"

"So I gave up my summer so you could get bored?"

I hadn't meant to say that. I really hadn't. The words had kind of exploded out, and I could tell Emma was shocked, too. She sort of reared back from the screen, blinking.

"What?"

"You let me take the fall for something *you* did so you could go to this dumb camp, and now you don't even like it anymore?"

Emma stared at me for a second, then said, "I didn't ask you to lie for me, Livvy."

"You didn't have to," I told her, sitting down in the grass. "You knew I wouldn't let you lose camp."

"I *didn't*," Emma insisted. She was sitting up now, and it was clear the phone was on her lap because she was sort of looming over the screen. "You always do this, you know," she went on. "You think everyone can read your mind, and we might be twins, Livvy, but I *can't read your mind*. And you go along with things without saying how you feel, and then you blame *me* for it! I took the lipstick to see if I could do it, and I felt really bad about it, and wish I hadn't, but *you're* the one who decided to say it was you. I never asked you to do that, and it isn't fair to blame me for it. Yes, I took the lipstick, and when I get home, I'll tell Mom, and I'm *sorry*."

Her voice was getting higher and squeakier, and she used her free hand to wipe at her eyes. Em always teared up when she got angry, something I knew she hated.

"But you should have said something *then*, Em," I said, feeling my own eyes sting. "And maybe you didn't ask me to, and maybe you're right that I don't tell people how I feel enough, but you make me feel like I'm . . . I don't know, holding you back or something."

And there it was, the thing I'd been scared to say to her: that I was afraid my own twin didn't like me all that much. She *loved* me, I knew that, but liking was something different.

"Oh, Livvy," Emma said on a sigh, sagging back against her bed and taking the phone with her. "You're not holding me back. I'm . . . I want to figure out how to be me without you sometimes, you know?"

I opened my mouth to say no, I didn't, and then I realized . . . I kind of did, actually.

I'd been angry at Emma, and feeling like this summer was all her fault, but I'd also had fun. I'd *been* fun. Ruby was a lot of things, but she was definitely honest, and I knew she hadn't pretended to think I was fun, that I was *funny*. At Camp Chrysalis, I'd been *Olivia* instead of *EmmaandOlivia*, and I'd liked it.

So I nodded. "Yeah," I said. "I do."

We were quiet, the sounds of the parade getting louder, and I glanced over my shoulder. The marching band had already passed by, but the majorettes were still coming, and I looked back at my phone.

"You wanna see some girls in sparkly costumes throw fire batons?" I asked, and Emma hesitated before smiling a little.

"Yeah," she said, "I really, really do."

And when I walked back toward the parade, I was smiling, too.

CHAPTER 28

RUBY

"Are we gonna go through the boxes today?"

My mom looked up from her spot at the kitchen table, where she was eating cereal and reading the newspaper. Her hair was up in a messy bun, and she was wearing her glasses. They had hot-pink frames to match the streak in her hair, just like my blue frames matched my hair. We'd gotten our glasses at the same time, and I still teased Mom about picking out ones from the kids' section. "Not my fault y'all get all the cool stuff," she'd said, and I couldn't argue with that. The adult glasses did look super boring.

"You mean Grammy's boxes?" Mom asked now, and I nodded.

That made Mom sit back. "Wow," she said. "Not even a joke about how, no, you meant Batman's boxes or the boxes by Narnia."

I was leaning against the door frame, which meant shrugging wasn't easy, but I still managed it.

And then Mom leaned forward, cupping her chin with one hand. "It's not a joking thing, I guess, is it?" she asked, and before I could say anything, she was standing up and pushing away from the table, the chair squeaking on the floor. "Yeah, let's do the boxes," Mom said. "And afterward, we'll go out for lunch, okay? Somewhere fun."

The boxes had sat in our garage for the past two months, ever since Grammy died. They were all that was left of her stuff. Mom had cleaned out the apartment, but all the furniture belonged there—Grammy had rented the place furnished because she said she didn't want to keep hauling boring things like couches and chairs to new houses.

But the apartment had been the last place she'd moved. She just hadn't known that.

It was weird, going out into the garage and looking at the boxes, knowing this was the last little thing we had to do to say good-bye to her. Mom must've felt the same, because she paused at the top of the brick steps leading down into the garage, putting her hand on my shoulder.

"This sucks, kid," she said, then added, "Don't repeat that."

"I won't," I promised. "But it does. A lot."

There were five boxes in all. Mom had meant to separate Grammy's things into types—you know, books here, pictures here, that kind of thing—but in the end, she'd put the stuff in boxes, saying we could sort it later. Which meant the first box I opened had three framed photographs, a stack of *Travel and Leisure* magazines, and four half-empty perfume bottles, plus a few little knickknacks. Salt and pepper shakers shaped like cows, a wireless speaker, a crochet angel that had probably gone on a Christmas tree at some point.

"Anything you want to keep, we keep," Mom said, kneeling over one of the other boxes.

That one was all books, and I nodded at it. "I want everything in there."

Mom didn't even look surprised or ask if I was sure. She nodded and shoved the box toward the steps up to the kitchen, then moved on to the third box.

It didn't take us very long to go through everything, which was such a weird feeling. Grammy had felt so . . . big. Not in her body—like me and Mom, she was a shrimp—but just *her*. The person she was had felt so full of life, so fun, and like her head was full of a million things. It didn't seem like all that *person* could be squeezed down into five boxes in a garage.

When we got to the last box, Mom sighed, pulling out a thick beige envelope. I could see my name scrawled across the front in bright blue pen, the familiar sight of Grammy's handwriting suddenly making me feel like crying in a way that nothing else in the boxes had. She always added all these loops and flourishes to my name, making it look bigger than it was. That's how she'd made me feel, too. Like *I* was bigger.

I took it, trying to keep my lips from trembling, but moms are too smart for that. "Rubes," she said softly, coming across the garage to hug me. As soon as my face was pressed into her shoulder, I felt the tears come, and I let them. I hadn't cried since the funeral because I hate crying. The snottiness, the wet face, the stinging in your eyes. But it felt good now, like a relief. Like I'd been holding on too tight to something.

Once I'd cried myself out, Mom and I sat there, cross-legged on the floor, facing each other with the envelope between us.

"Do you want to read it?" Mom asked, her voice gentle, and I looked at the letter, thinking. I did, but it was like the boxes—it felt like the *end* of something, the last thing from Grammy I was ever going to read, and that was harder than I'd thought it would be. But in the end, I wanted to know what it said too much to save it for another time, and I figured I might as well get this all done with at once. Like ripping off a Band-Aid.

So I picked up the envelope, gently opened it, and read:

> *Rubes,*
>
> *It feels so silly leaving a letter for you like this, like I don't talk to you and see your sweet face every day. But there are some things it's easier to say in a letter, I suppose, and I never wanted us to talk about what was happening, how I might not be around much longer. Honestly, I'm not scared to go, but I sure will miss you, Ruby Sue. (And yes, I know that's not your actual middle name, but it should've been, and I like it, and this is my last letter to you, so there.)*
>
> *I think we're very lucky in that we've probably said everything there is to say to each other over the past few years. You know I love you, and I know you love me. I know that might not seem all that unusual, but believe me, there are a lot of people in this world who don't get*

that. So I'm not going to be sad, because I had the best granddaughter in the whole world, and I made sure she knew it.

So don't be sad, sugar. Listen to your mama, be sweet, and please, please, please keep being you. You are funny and smart and the world needs more people who know who they are as well as you do.

A few last-minute things:

1) The next time you dye your hair, try purple. I think it would look so pretty with your coloring.

2) Make your mom try that internet dating site again. I know that Fish Guy was a disaster, but she's gotta keep trying.

3) Whenever you pass a fountain, throw a penny in. Unless that's not allowed, then don't do that.

4) Actually, do it anyway, but try not to get caught.

5) Check the root cellar.

6) Honestly, I don't know what that last one means, but I woke up the other night with "Tell Ruby to check the root cellar" in my head, so there you go.

7) Don't change one little thing about yourself, Ruby Sue. You are unique and brave and beautiful, and I love you so much,

Grammy

After I'd read it a second time, I handed it over to Mom, who was also looking a little teary. She took it, her eyes moving over the page. She smiled, but it wobbled a little, and then, when she got to the list, she frowned. "Fish Guy?"

"That guy who liked that one band so much," I reminded her.

"Oh, *Phish* Guy."

She handed the letter back to me. "I wonder what she meant about the root cellar."

Shrugging, I gently folded the letter up and put it back in its envelope. "You know how Grammy always said she was a little bit psychic, but over random things."

"We don't even *have* a root cellar," Mom said, standing up and dusting her hands on her jeans before offering me a hand up.

I took it, letting her pull me to my feet, but as she did, something occurred to me.

No, we definitely did not have a root cellar.

But Live Oak House probably did.

LivAndLetLiv: Hi.

RubyToozday: Hi?

LivAndLetLiv: It's me. Liv. I got a new username.

RubyToozday: I picked up on that.

RubyToozday: ;)

RubyToozday: I saw you at the parade the other night. You were on your phone?

LivAndLetLiv: Oh, yeah. Talking to Emma.

LivAndLetLiv: Well, fighting with Emma.

LivAndLetLiv: But it's good now? At least I think it is. I don't know, it's weird.

RubyToozday: Kind of going around lately, isn't it?

RubyToozday: The Weird.

RubyToozday: Sorry, that was me trying to make this NOT weird, and failing.

RubyToozday: And also I'm sorry in a general sense.

RubyToozday: About Mrs. Freely's office and being bossy about it.

RubyToozday: I am a bossy monster.

RubyToozday: Hello?

LivAndLetLiv: I like how you talk too much even when you're NOT talking.

LivAndLetLiv: :)

RubyToozday: Diarrhea of the mouth AND of the fingers!

LivAndLetLiv: EWWWWWWW!!

RubyToozday: BUT YOU LAUGHED I BET.

LivAndLetLiv: I DID NOT.

RubyToozday: YOU DID I SENSED IT I SENSED THE LAUGH THROUGH THE COMPUTER AND OUR FRIENDSHIP BOND.

RubyToozday: I mean. If we are still friends?

LivAndLetLiv: We are.

LivAndLetLiv: Real friends argue sometimes, right?

LivAndLetLiv: Yo Yo Yo tomorrow?

RubyToozday: Yo.

RubyToozday: By which I mean YES.

CHAPTER 29

OLIVIA

We met at Yo Yo Yo again, my mom dropping me off while she went to go do some shopping. I wasn't sure if Ruby's mom had taken her or if she'd ridden her bike, but she was already in the shop when I walked in the door, sitting at the same back table we'd chosen the last time we were there. She already had her cup of yogurt, and I could see the mound of sprinkles from where I stood.

I got my own cup and filled it with cookies-and-cream yogurt, a dollop of brownie batter, and finished it off with white chocolate cheesecake. Then I got a little scoop of every sugary topping they had, covered the whole thing in whipped cream and caramel sauce, and went to pay.

It was the most expensive yogurt I'd ever bought, but the look on Ruby's face when I came to the table made it more than worth it.

"Respect," she said solemnly, eyeing the monstrosity I'd concocted.

"I can't eat all of this," I told her, and she shook her head.

"No, that's really something you should just admire rather than eat," Ruby agreed, and I laughed, sticking my spoon in anyway.

For a little while, we ate in silence. The last time we'd talked in person, we'd argued, and while we'd apologized for all that on chat, that had been *typing*, not talking. This felt different and a little weird.

Ruby finally sighed and set her neon-green spoon on the napkin by her nearly empty cup of yogurt. "This is awkward," she said, and I felt kind of relieved.

"Super awkward," I agreed, and Ruby sighed again.

"Can we maybe have a whole do-over on everything?" she asked. "Forget the rest of the summer and start fresh?"

I thought that over and, after a second, shook my head. "No, because sometimes friends argue. It's over now, but we can't pretend it didn't happen. That's . . . part of being friends."

Ruby looked at me with an expression I'd never seen on her face before. It was almost . . . serious. When was Ruby Kaye *ever* serious?

"So we are friends," she said at last, and I felt my cheeks go hot.

"Of course we are," I said. "We've had yogurt and hunted ghosts together. What do you call that if not friendship?"

Ruby grinned. "One messed-up summer."

That made me laugh, and I drew a little spiral in my whipped cream with the tip of my spoon. "It's been that, too," I agreed. "But it's . . . I don't know, it's been fun. Scary and yeah, messed up, but . . . fun. Which is a weird thing to admit."

Ruby gave a shrug, sitting back in her chair and picking up her spoon again. "Sometimes fun should be weird," she said, and now she looked and sounded more like the Ruby I was used to.

"I feel like all your fun is weird," I told her, and she made a fake-outraged sound.

That got me giggling again, and for a while, we sat there and talked about normal stuff—I told her about the fight with Em, and Ruby told me about cleaning out the boxes from her grandmother's apartment, and that it hadn't been as sad as she'd thought it would be.

"Look at us," I said, pushing away my cup of yogurt even though I'd only had a few bites. "We both did hard, scary things, and they ended up not being that hard or that scary."

"Once you've spent time cleaning a carnivorous house, I guess most things are easy and not scary," Ruby said, and then she leaned forward in her seat, folding her arms on the sticky plastic table.

"If I say something that sounds kind of crazy, do you promise not to judge me?"

I sat back in my chair, the plastic squeaking a little, and gave Ruby my best version of her own "are you kidding me?" look.

"Rube," I said. "Ruby Tuesday. Rubik's Cube."

Her eyes lit up. "Omigosh, that's a good one," she said, dimples appearing in her cheeks. "Please call me that forever, I *love* it." Then she shook her head. "Okay, stupid question, I know. We're deep into Crazy Town these days, so what's a little extra weird?"

With that, she turned around and got the bag that had been hanging off the back of her chair, fishing around in it until she pulled out an envelope.

"Here."

She handed it to me, and as soon as I saw the pretty handwriting on the front, I looked up at her, eyebrows raised. "Is this—"

"From my grammy, yeah. Read it."

I did. I was sad then that I'd never gotten to know Ruby's grammy, because from this letter she seemed pretty great, and it was clear she had loved Ruby a lot.

"She was awesome," I said quietly, and one corner of Ruby's mouth kicked up slightly.

"She was, but that's not why I wanted you to read it. Check item five."

"'Check the root cellar,'" I read, then looked up at Ruby, frowning. "What does that mean?"

Ruby nodded at the letter in my hand. "Grammy always swore she was a little bit psychic. Not for big things, just the little stuff, but still. It has to mean the house, right?"

Chewing my lower lip, I looked up at the giant TV over us. The lady was adding a bunch of flour to a giant glass bowl now, talking happily about something, her mouth moving but no sound coming out. "Is there a root cellar?" I asked at last, and Ruby shrugged.

"It's a big house," she reminded me. "Not too hard to believe it might have one of those."

We sat there for a while, thinking.

"Sooo," I said slowly. "We could go back to Live Oak House tomorrow and check out this root cellar, and possibly get caught by Mrs. Freely *again*."

Ruby shrugged. "A risk, yes."

I bit my lower lip, still tasting a little bit of caramel there, thinking it over.

If I said no, it might hurt her feelings. This was a letter from her grammy, after all, and we had just made up from the last fight. What if turning this down made Ruby decide she didn't want to be friends after all?

But then I remembered talking to Emma on the Fourth of July, Emma saying that she'd thought everything was fine because I never *said* what I really wanted, and I went along with it.

Pushing back my shoulders, I looked Ruby in the eye. "I really don't want to," I told her. "Because I'm worried about getting in trouble at school."

Other words were right there on the tip of my tongue, stuff about how I knew that was dumb, or that if she wanted to do it, I understood, but I kept them back. I was done explaining or talking myself down.

I didn't want to go into the root cellar, and I wasn't going to.

And Ruby smiled. "Fair enough!" she said cheerfully, gathering up her yogurt stuff.

"Just like that?" I said, blinking.

She gave another shrug, sitting back in her chair. "You don't want to. People shouldn't have to do things they don't want to do, and hey, it's probably the smartest idea."

Balling up her napkin, Ruby tossed it to the trash. "We're hanging up our ghost-hunting shoes."

CHAPTER 30

RUBY

"Look at us," I said to Olivia the next day as we clambered out of the van at the road in front of Live Oak House. "Turning over a new leaf, being responsible campers at Camp Chrysalis."

"It actually feels kind of strange," Liv said once her feet hit the hard-packed dirt. "Coming here to . . . do what we're supposed to."

I nodded and dusted my hands off on the back of my pants. "Our ghost-hunting days are over."

"Your what?" Garrett asked. I hadn't noticed him coming up to stand behind us, and I jumped a little. We hadn't talked much since the whole bite thing—I think it had really freaked him out—and my face burned hot all of a sudden.

"Just. You know. How me and Olivia were goofing off," I told him. "Acting like there were ghosts in this place. Like your *vroom-vroom* head."

Garrett tilted his head to one side, then gave a little laugh. "You're a weird kid," he told me before jogging off to catch up with the others.

I could feel Olivia's eyes on me, but I said, "Been called worse," before trudging after everyone else to go up to the house.

Once we were all assembled in the front hallway, Mrs. Freely did her whole "daily giving out of assignments" thing, and I was so busy still thinking about what Garrett had said that I almost missed it when she said, "And Ruby and Olivia, the doll room."

Jerking my head, I turned to face her more fully. "Excuse?"

Mrs. Freely looked at me over the top of her clipboard. "The doll room," she repeated. "We've been putting that one off since you were all so *funny* about it."

"Terrified," I corrected her. "We were terrified because it's a room filled with creepy dolls."

"They're not creepy, they're antiques," Mrs. Freely said. "And they have to be done. We've put it off long enough."

This was it, I realized. Our punishment for sneaking into the office. We were getting off lightly, really—like Mrs. Freely had said, there were real consequences for screwing up at Camp Chrysalis, scary *school* consequences, and we weren't getting those.

We were just getting fed to dolls.

Nope, nope, none of that, *new leaf.*

"Sounds good," I made myself say, and once again, I could feel Olivia looking at me.

It had been cloudy that morning, and the day seemed even darker as we made our way over to the room full of dolls, notebooks in hand.

And when I opened the door, I realized that the room was even creepier than I'd remembered.

Still dolls everywhere, big ones, little ones, expensive porcelain ones, and plainer rag dolls.

Next to me, Olivia shuddered. "Let's get this over with."

"I'm really glad we're not ghost-hunting anymore, by the way," I told her, opening up my notebook. "Because if we were—"

"But we're not," Olivia replied firmly, and I nodded.

"But we're not."

I moved to the nearest display case of dolls, jotting down *Redheaded doll, messed-up smile, lacy dress*, and hoped that would be a good enough description. I wasn't sure how specific they wanted us to be on the dolls, and since there were so many, I felt like I'd start running out of descriptions if I wasn't careful.

Liv was on the other side of the room, writing a lot on her notebook, and I smiled at her. "You actually like this, don't you?"

Lifting her head, she wrinkled her nose at me. "Not the dolls themselves, really, but working with you is nice. Especially since we're being normal."

"Noooorrrrmaaaaal," I echoed, tapping my pen against my notebook. "That is us. Responsible humans, doing the job we were assigned like bosses."

"Total bosses," Liv confirmed, and I turned back to my work with a smile.

Trying to figure out The Spooky at Live Oak House had been fun, but this was nice, too, just hanging out with Liv.

Putting down my notebook, I picked up the doll nearest to me, a smaller one that wasn't nearly as fancy as some of the others, dressed in a simple blue calico dress. Its hair was made from yellow yarn, and it had a bright smile painted on its porcelain face. She was still a *little* unsettling—she was a doll, after all—but not as bad as some of the others. Maybe because there wasn't any rouge painted on her cheeks.

"Hi, Olivia!" I said in a high voice. "I'm Sally, the one non-nightmare doll, saaaaave meeeee!"

Giggling, Olivia put her own notebook down and folded her arms over her chest. "Sorry, Sally, it's your destiny to remain in the creepy doll room forever."

, I lifted both of Sally's arms in the air. "Nooooo!" I cried in the high voice. "Curse you, fates!"

"Wish I could help, Sal, but them's the breaks," Liv answered, shrugging, and I grinned at her, going to set Sally down.

"Help us," Sally said.

Olivia threw her hands up. "Sally, I told you—"

"Liv," I said, and the word came out like a croak.

She immediately dropped her hands, a little V forming between her brows. "What?"

I stared down at the doll, my whole body suddenly freezing cold, my breath coming so fast, I was almost panting. "I didn't," I managed to get out. "I didn't say that."

Olivia stood up straighter, her face suddenly pale. "Ruby, come on," she said, and I looked at her, widening my eyes.

"Liv, I know I like to joke, but I promise you, this is not a thing I would joke about. *I didn't say that.*"

We stood there, staring at "Sally" where she lay on the little table, her painted face smiling up at the ceiling. It was bright in the doll room, the sun pouring in through the big windows, the light moving through the lace curtains to make fancy patterns on the floor, but Liv and I stood very still, almost holding our breath.

And then it came again, faint, but still clear. "Help me."

I backed up from the doll so fast that I slammed into one of the other tables, knocking dolls off their stands and to the floor. Olivia stood in the middle of the room, her mouth open, and then it was like the sounds were all around us, a storm of whispers.

Help us help us help us slithered around the room, the words overlapping, and I couldn't tell if it was more than one person talking or the same voice repeating and repeating.

Spinning in a circle, I looked at all the dolls, their blank smiles, their overly bright hair, the lace dresses, the linen nightgowns, some small enough to hold in one hand, some nearly as tall as an actual toddler. They weren't moving, but it was like each of them was murmuring to us, and I fought the urge to cover my ears with my hands.

And then the words changed, but slowly. Some of the voices still seemed to be saying *Help us*, but there were other words sliding in and around them now.

The cellar the cellar the cellar.

My eyes met Liv's across the room, and I saw my own shock reflected in her face. She was hearing it, too: *The cellar.*

Just like Grammy's note had said.

And then the words started to slur so that *cellar* became almost more like a hiss, a sort of constant *sssssssss*, rising and rising, and then I did put my hands over my ears, the notebook falling from my fingers.

Just when I thought I might snap and scream or start crying or *something*, the sounds suddenly stopped, leaving Liv and me standing on opposite sides of the room, breathing hard, nearly shaking.

"You guys okay?"

I did scream then—okay, to be honest, it was more like a yelp—and turned to see Wesley standing in the doorway, his hair, as usual, hanging over his eyes. I swallowed hard, walking closer to him.

"How long have you been standing there?"

He swung his head from one side to the other, and I realized that underneath his hair, he was looking from me to Olivia and back again. And then he shrugged.

Great. Back to the silent treatment.

"Wesley," Olivia asked, coming to stand next to me. "Did you . . . did you hear anything?"

And while Wesley didn't actually say anything, his head-shake—no—was all the answer we needed.

RubyToozday: So we need to get back into Live Oak House, but we need to do it at a time when no one else will be there.

LivAndLetLiv: Hi to you, too, Ruby.

RubyToozday: We can't have formalities when dealing with talking dolls, Liv.

LivAndLetLiv: I guess that's a good point.

RubyToozday: Tomorrow night work for you?

LivAndLetLiv: WHAT???????

LivAndLetLiv: Ruby, we can't sneak out of our houses and INTO a house at night. That's a CRIMINAL THING. We TALKED about this.

RubyToozday: WE ARE KIDS. We can say it was a dare or something, that we're dumb, whatever. I really want to get a look in that root cellar, okay?

RubyToozday: Grammy said to look in there. The dolls said to look in there.

RubyToozday: So we gotta look.

LivAndLetLiv: And how are we going to get in there at night?

RubyToozday: Garrett said he could get the key for us.

LivAndLetLiv: You told GARRETT?

RubyToozday: You gotta stop capslocking me, Liv. And yes, I did, because we'll need HELP. (CAPSLOCKED YOU BACK.)

LivAndLetLiv: What did you tell him?

RubyToozday: The basics. Talking dolls, attic creepiness, possible killer tree.

RubyToozday: Told him to be PREPARED FOR ANYTHING.

LivAndLetLiv: This is crazy, Ruby.

RubyToozday: Not really! We're gonna go in, have a little look around, see what's what, then decide if we should burn down the house or not!

LivAndLetLiv: Ruby.

LivAndLetLiv: No.

LivAndLetLiv: We are NOT burning down the house.

RubyToozday: Even for TALKING DOLLS, LIV?

LivAndLetLiv: Even for that. Also, we need to stop typing all this out in case someone sees. Can you call me?

RubyToozday: On it!

CHAPTER 31

RUBY

Later, I would think about how it was kind of funny—ironic, I guess—that the things that had gotten me and Olivia sent to Camp Chrysalis for the summer were nowhere near as bad as the thing we did *because* we'd been sent to Camp Chrysalis for the summer.

Honestly, someone should tell Mrs. Freely.

Before Camp Chrysalis? I threw some glitter (okay, a *lot* of glitter) in a school hallway.

After Camp Chrysalis? Let's break it down:

I rifled through someone else's things in a sneaky manner.

I accused an adult of trying to feed us to a murder house.

I told multiple fibs to my mom.

The abovementioned sneaking-out thing.

Being out at night with a boy.

And as Garrett, Liv, and I stopped our bikes on the road at the base of Live Oak House, I reminded myself that if we got caught, we wouldn't be looking at Camp Chrysalis but probably military school. Maybe juvie. Was that still a thing people got sent to?

We parked our bikes and got off, heading up toward the house. I had brought a bag even though there was nothing in it except a flashlight and a bag of Chex Mix.

Garrett had a bag, too, but Liv was empty-handed except for her own flashlight.

Once we were on the lawn, the three of us stood there, our flashlights in our hands but not turned on, staring at the house rising up in front of us. We'd been coming here for weeks, and we'd known how scary the house was almost that whole time, but it was still different being in the house in the daylight, lots of people around us, and being here at night, with Live Oak House looming out of the darkness, the branches of the oak out front making spooky shadows.

Or maybe I was freaked out because we were about to do something that would get us into a lot of trouble.

"Ready?" I whispered, and I clutched my flashlight harder, feeling it slip against my sweaty palm.

"Ready," Olivia replied.

There was silence, and we both glanced over at Garrett, still standing between us, staring up at the house with wide eyes.

"Garrett?" I prompted, and I could actually see him swallow hard. We hadn't talked about the whole bite thing, really, but maybe it had bothered him more than he'd said? And then he shook his head as he shoved his flashlight back into his bag and turned away.

"No way," he muttered. "No way no way no way, this is not cool."

And with that, he shoved his bag into my hands, nearly

making me drop my flashlight. "Here," he said. "The key is in the front pocket, and there's some other stuff you might need, but I'm . . . yeah, no."

He started backing away from the house, and I stared at him in shock. "Are you *serious?*" I whispered.

He just turned around and started running. I could hear his footsteps pounding away, and as he reached his bike at the bottom of the hill, he didn't even bother to look at us. He slung his backpack over a shoulder, got on his bike, and pedaled off, leaving me and Ruby staring after him.

"Ugghhhhh," I groaned. "Well, that crush is totally over."

Olivia turned back to me, raising her eyebrows. "I thought you said you didn't have a crush on him."

I waved my hands as I turned to the house. "Um, of course I had a crush on him."

"But you said—" she started, and I shot her a look over my shoulder.

"Liv, can we not right now? What with the monster house and all?"

"Right," she agreed quickly, moving to stand closer to me. "Eyes on the prize."

"Exactly."

"And the prize is a terrifying house that might eat us."

"You know it."

We stood like that for a while, staring up at Live Oak House. I really think until that moment it hadn't hit us what we were trying to do. We were walking into a house we knew was bad.

Haunted. "It's not going to get any less scary," I finally said. "No matter how long we stand here."

"Are we sure about that?" Liv asked.

The night was warm—hot, really, without even a breeze to cool things down—and I could feel sweat slithering down my back. A mosquito was buzzing around my head, and I swatted at it, thinking I probably should've grabbed some Off along with my flashlight.

I turned and looked at Liv. In the dim moonlight, she was even paler than usual, and her eyes seemed huge in her face. "We don't have to do this," I said, and I was surprised to find I really meant it.

That for all the time we'd spent working out how to fix this, how to *stop* it, if Liv had said she wanted to go home, I would've packed up my flashlight and we could've gone home.

That, more than anything else that had happened, reminded me that Olivia Anne Willingham was most definitely my friend.

And since she was *my* friend, she shook her head and said, "No. Let's finish this."

I grinned and held out my fist. "Bump it."

She did, and then, together, we walked toward the house.

I fished the key Garrett had gotten for me out of his bag as we walked up the porch steps, the wood creaking underfoot. It sounded too loud in the night, and I had a sudden vision of police cars swarming up the road, somehow magically alerted that me and Olivia Willingham were up here, very firmly up to no good.

But there were no cars, no lights or sirens, and when I put

the key in the lock, there wasn't even a squeal of protest from the door. If anything, it sagged open with something like a sigh.

Like it had been waiting for us.

Okay, no, that was too creepy a thought, and I shoved it away as quickly as I could, pushing my shoulders back and flipping my flashlight on. The beam illuminated the hall that I was so familiar with, and I found myself pointing it toward the spot where we usually met in the morning to get all our supplies. There, right at the base of the staircase, that one tree trunk soaring up through the ceiling overhead.

"This is so crazy," Olivia whispered next to me. "This thing we're doing, it is *crazy*."

At the beginning of the summer, Liv would've said that like it was a bad thing. Her lips would have been clamped together, and there would've been a wrinkle between her brows. Now she said it a little breathlessly, and when I looked back over at her, she wasn't smiling, but there was something in her face that told me that while yes, she thought this was super scary, she was having fun, too.

Which maybe made *her* the weird one in this friendship.

We crept along the floor, heading for the back hallway. It was weird how being here at night made everything feel so different. If I'd thought the house was scary during the day, that was nothing compared to now. All that stuff we'd spent the summer cataloging cast its own shadows. Big ones, little ones, dark shapes all over the place, and there was just *so* much dark. With a house this big, there were parts the moonlight couldn't reach through the windows, rooms so big and hallways so long, my flashlight beam couldn't reach all the way.

And, as I now *knew*, there were freaking *talking dolls in here*.

Yeah, not the time for that thought.

I'd never been down this little hallway before, and it was so narrow, I wasn't sure anyone much bigger than me or Olivia *could* have made it down.

"I wondered where this led," Olivia whispered. "I saw it a few weeks ago but didn't check it out."

"I can't imagine why," I whispered back, even though there really wasn't any need for us to be quiet. "It's not like it's terrifying or anything."

There was a door at the end of the hall, and we both slowed down as we approached. My heart seemed to have climbed up my throat and into my mouth, and I reached for the doorknob.

It didn't turn.

The cellar door was locked.

CHAPTER 32

OLIVIA

Ruby rattled the doorknob again, and I crouched down, shining my flashlight on the doorjamb.

"It's a padlock," I told her, reaching out with my free hand to touch it.

Sighing, Ruby stepped back. "Great. I didn't even think about that. I bet Mrs. Freely doesn't have a key for that, so—what are you doing?"

I had gotten back up and was opening the second bag slung on Ruby's back, the one Garrett had brought. He probably had something—aha!

Smiling, I pulled a wrench from the bag, and Ruby stared at me. It was maybe the first time I'd ever seen her look genuinely shocked.

"We can break it with this," I said, and to be honest, I was a little shocked myself. But we had come this far, and we were risking a *lot* to be here.

I wasn't ready to turn back now.

"This is bad," Ruby whispered, even as she steadied the

flashlight on the door in front of her. "Like, *really* bad. Glitter is one thing, but breaking down a locked door?"

My palms were sweating, and my chest felt tight, my skin tingly. But still, I lifted the wrench, smiled at Ruby, and said, "We're Bad Kids, right?"

And with that, I brought the wrench down on the lock—hard.

I had never broken anything on purpose in my life, and I wasn't even sure any of this would work, but the lock was old and rusted, and maybe I aimed it the right way, or maybe—and I would think about this for a long time after everything was over—maybe the house had wanted to let me in. Me and Ruby both.

For us to find its last secret.

The lock fell to the floor with a thump, rusty flakes floating in the flashlight's beam, and the cellar door creaked open slowly.

"That could not have been more horror movie," Ruby whispered. "There's probably zombies in there."

"Hey, Ruby?" I whispered back. "Can you not right now?"

"Sorry," Ruby answered, and I thought she sounded genuinely contrite until she added, "But when I build this house in Minecraft, I'm putting Creepers down here."

Ignoring that, I stepped forward and pushed on the door. As intense as it had seemed when we first found it, I'd almost expected to have to really shove, bracing myself for the shrieking of metal. But the door almost felt light when I pushed it the rest of the way open.

I thought about the way the front door had opened, too, so easily, and it made me swallow hard.

Was the house letting us in only to trap us?

A scent drifted out of the cellar as the door swung back, and Ruby stepped back, putting her arm across her face. The bag Garrett had handed her swung down to her elbow. "Eugh." She shuddered. "What is that?"

I shook my head, my brain trying to make sense of it. Part of it was the sort of earthy smell of dirt and growing things. That was nice, reminding me of my mom's little flower garden in the backyard, spring afternoons helping her plant impatiens and pansies. But underneath, there was a different, sweeter scent, like something rotting, and it seemed to curl up around us, sliding into our noses and making both of us stand there, frozen, unable to walk forward.

"I think that's the house," I heard myself say, the beam of the flashlight wavering on the steps leading down into the cellar. "Like . . . that's what's gone bad here."

"A bunch of groceries rotting?" Ruby asked, arm still pressed to her face, so her words were muffled. "Because that's for sure what it smells like."

She shivered again, but then she lowered her arm, readjusted her bags, and took one step onto the top step, the wood creaking underneath her foot. "Okay," she said, and I felt like maybe she was talking to herself more than to me. "We have not broken into a house just to be scared off by a bad smell. We are going down there."

"We are," I agreed, but I couldn't seem to make my foot take that first step the way Ruby had.

Then she reached behind her, her cold fingers curling around my wrist, tugging me forward. "As long as we don't get scared at the same time, I think we can do this," she said, and despite the awful smell wafting up from the cellar and the darkness of the house (and the mind-blowing wrongness of what we were doing), I smiled.

"I think we're both pretty scared right now?"

Ruby paused and glanced over her shoulder at me, angling so that the beam of the flashlight wasn't in her face. "Yeah, but I mean *really* scared. That whole frozen terror. You can do that sometimes, and *I* can do that sometimes, but we for sure cannot do that at the same time or this won't get done. So you can be super scared right now, and I'll be brave, and then later, if I get super scared—"

"I'll be the brave one," I said. "I got it."

"Friendship!" Ruby said, raising her free hand in a fist, and I chuckled, shaking my head.

"You're so weird."

But it had made me feel better, joking with Ruby, so that I'd moved down the steps without even thinking about it, really, the light of my flashlight pretty steady.

"We're right under the tree," Ruby went on, "or trunk, whatever. I wonder if it goes all the way into the ground down here."

I could've turned my flashlight to the side to see, but even if I wasn't feeling as terrified right now, I wanted to keep the light right in front of me. What if I looked over to the side and then something came rushing up the cellar stairs?

Okay, that was a bad thought, a Very Not Good Thought, one I for sure should not have had.

Ruby stopped, looking back at me. "Frozen in terror?" she asked, squinting slightly.

I gave a quick nod. "Just for a sec," I promised. "Suddenly pictured someone—"

"AH!" Ruby exclaimed, holding up her hand, palm out. "No, no, no. I am being the brave one right now, remember? Any scary images, you keep them to yourself, because capital-N Nope."

I closed my eyes quickly, sucking in a deep breath through my mouth so I wouldn't have to smell so much of that icky, rotten smell. "Gotcha," I said. "No sharing the scary."

"Exactly." Ruby moved forward again, and the steps kept creaking. I focused on that sound, how everything was so quiet except for our footsteps. That meant we were alone.

Then, as we got close to the bottom of the steps, I saw something that made me pull up short, Ruby's fingers sliding on my wrist.

"What is—" she started, but as I panned the flashlight up, her words died in her throat, turning into something a little bit like a squeak.

There were . . . *things* hanging from the ceiling. For a second, I had a bizarre memory of learning about stalactites and stalagmites in third grade. *These are stalactites,* my confused brain thought, *because they're hanging* tight *to the ceiling.*

But this wasn't a cave, and those weren't rocks.

It was Ruby who finally found the courage to say it out loud.

"They're *roots*."

CHAPTER 33

RUBY

I stared up at the ceiling of the root cellar, and there was a part of me that almost wanted to laugh.

Root cellar was definitely the right term for this place, but staring up at all those straggling things hanging from the ceiling suddenly made me think of snakes or fingers reaching out for me, big, fat, dirt-covered fingers, and wow, I really hoped Liv was feeling brave right now because I was definitely *not*.

"It's *growing*," she breathed, spinning around, her flashlight beam bouncing off the sea of roots above us. "I mean, I knew it was a tree and all, and that makes sense, but . . . I guess I thought the roots would be in the ground? Why are they . . . hanging here? That's—"

"Both scientifically impossible and also super creepy," I said. Or croaked, actually.

Then I shook my head, making my numb fingers reach into my pocket to pull out my phone. "Okay. Okay. Okay."

"Stop saying that," Liv whispered, and I shook my head again, my hair sticking to sweaty places on my face even though I was covered in goose bumps.

"If I say it enough, maybe it'll be true," I told her, then hissed as my phone tumbled from my suddenly numb fingers and landed on the dirt floor. Crouching down, I fumbled for it, and as I did, something *moved* near my hand.

I shrieked, pulling back so fast that I overbalanced and fell backward, my butt landing hard on the floor, and Olivia's flashlight swung wildly in my direction, the beam wobbling.

"Ruby?" she called, and I made myself laugh even though it sounded kind of breathless and weird.

"I'm fine," I called back. "Just clumsy and freaked out."

Maybe nothing had moved by my hand after all, I told myself. Maybe I was being silly, and—

The root shot out of the dirt fast as a snake, and I didn't even have time to think before it wrapped around my ankle, squeezing.

Hard.

If I had been creeped out before, I was now terrified, so scared I couldn't even shout, my mouth opening and closing, but no sound coming out.

And there was a part of my mind saying this couldn't be happening, I could *not* be under attack from some kind of killer tree in the cellar of an old house!

Okay, so panic was definitely happening, and I made a sobbing noise, kicking at the root with my other foot as Liv dashed over, dropping her flashlight and sinking to her knees.

And then she did one of the bravest things I've ever seen anyone do—she actually *grabbed* the root with both her hands, pulling hard.

It didn't do any good, though, and the root tightened even more, tugging me down. Toward what?

I wasn't sure I wanted to know.

There was another rumbling sound then, and as I watched, another root shot out, grabbing Liv's wrist.

She shrieked, and I found myself reaching for her, my fingers brushing the edge of her shirt, but I couldn't hold on. The roots were tugging us, even as we both struggled, reaching for each other, reaching for anything, and they kept pulling. The cellar was full of that rotting smell, of loose dirt, of the sounds of both of us shrieking, and then, finally, my hand caught Olivia's. Our fingers interlocked, palms sweating, and then suddenly, everything went dark.

We're hiding in the hollow of the tree.

It's our special place, the one place on this whole farm that is only ours, and Ma and Pa never come bother us when we're out here. Neither does Lucy, but then, Lucy has not paid much attention to us since Felix came to work on the farm.

Lucy loves Felix, but we do not. His hair is too bright and his eyes are too cold, and sometimes he looks at everything—Lucy, the farm—as though it belongs to him.

He doesn't like us, either, and says we are sneaky just because we catch him and Lucy kissing in the barn.

But being sneaky is how you learn. No one tells us anything, so if we didn't sneak, we wouldn't know.

Wouldn't know that Felix and Lucy meant to run away together.

Wouldn't know that Pa found out and forbade it.

Wouldn't know that even though Pa told Felix to leave and never come back, he did come back, in the night, like he was the sneaky one.

We saw. Saw him creep around the side of the house, saw Lucy's window open. We didn't tell Ma and Pa, because we might be sneaks, but we aren't tattles.

What we don't see is the fire.

We don't know how it starts. Did Lucy knock over a lantern on her way out? Was Felix worse than a sneak, a monster who wanted to make sure there was no one left to come after him and Lucy?

We don't know. We only remember the sudden thick, choking smoke. The way our chests ache with it.

We help each other because that's what we've always done, but we are already weak, our lungs full of smoke, and the night is so cold.

When we stumble into our hiding place, we clutch each other, trying to breathe even though it's hard, even though the frost underfoot stings our bare feet. Our nightgowns are thin. Our bodies are too small. But inside the tree, inside our special hiding place, we almost feel warm.

It's so easy to go to sleep here, holding each other.

And we stay here. It takes us a while to notice that something is strange, that we don't feel the same as we once did, and that leaving the tree is not possible. But that's all right. We have each other.

And later, when Felix and Lucy come back, Felix in a nice suit like nothing we'd ever seen him wear before, our sister at his side in a white dress, we whisper to them.

Maybe they don't hear us, but when the time comes to build their fancy new house far away from these mountains, Lucy tells Felix to take our tree. That our tree will come with them to their new home, be a part of their new house. Maybe she remembers our special hiding place and wants to remember us.

She doesn't know that she brings us, too.

Bad things happen when we get to our new home. Things we try not to remember. But those things—the bad ones, with the breaking chains and the shouts and the terrible crunching sound—seem to make us stronger. We are still tied to our tree, but it is in the house now, nestled deep inside, which means that we are in the house, too.

Watching. Learning. Sneaking.

We don't like the new house. We don't like Felix and his cold eyes. We don't know how the fire started, but when we look at all these things Felix buys for himself and remember the money Pa had once hidden in the woods by our home, we wonder.

And the longer we wonder, the angrier we get, because we should not still be in this tree, and we do not want to spend forever in a place that Felix built.

So we wait.

And grow stronger.

And grow.

And wait.

We love each other but sometimes wish there were other people to play with. There is a boy once, but he is frightened of us, and he grows up into a man, and then the house is empty again.

Then, suddenly, noise.

Other children.

People to play with.

Girls who are lonely like us.

And we don't have to wait anymore.

I came back to myself, gasping, the voices still echoing in my head. High, sweet voices. Little-girl voices.

Rebecca and Octavia.

"The twins!" Olivia called out next to me, and even though the roots had stopped pulling, they were still holding tight to me.

Olivia, however, had somehow wiggled free, and she sat on the ground, breathing hard, her hands dirty and shaking as she brought them up to push her hair off her face. "Felix wasn't a Wrexhall," she breathed. "They were. He married their sister and took their name—"

"And probably murdered the rest of them, yeah," I panted back, still struggling. "And now they're seriously angry little-girl ghosts inside a killer tree, so yay, mystery solved, now *get me out of here.*"

Shaking herself slightly, Liv got back up on her knees and reached for my hand.

And then the roots yanked again, harder this time, and I actually screamed.

"Garrett's bag!" I yelled at Liv.

Who knew if he'd actually brought anything that would help, but it seemed like it was worth a try, and when the ground beneath us began to shake, I added, "And hurry!"

Liv didn't have to be told twice. She snatched up the bag

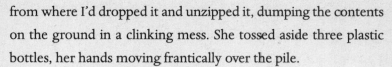

from where I'd dropped it and unzipped it, dumping the contents on the ground in a clinking mess. She tossed aside three plastic bottles, her hands moving frantically over the pile.

And then she gave a cry and hefted a small hatchet.

Garrett was clearly hardcore.

I swallowed hard, still kicking at the root holding me, as Liv moved back over to my side.

As I stared up at her, standing over me with a hatchet in her hand, I was suddenly very glad that we had become friends this summer. Otherwise, Olivia Anne Willingham coming after me with a weapon would've been almost as scary as a killer tree wrapping around me.

"Do it, Liv!" I shouted as she stared down at me, her face white in the glow from the flashlight, her chest heaving, she was breathing so hard.

"What if I cut you?" she replied, but then the root yanked on me again, and I screamed, my fingers digging into the dirt.

That was clearly what decided it for Liv.

The hatchet came down, and I squeezed my eyes shut, half expecting to feel the bite of metal on my skin. I loved Olivia, and she was my friend, but I wasn't sure I'd be able to forgive her if she chopped my foot off.

There was a *thunk* and a shriek, but it didn't come from me, and then the pressure was suddenly off my ankle.

My eyes flew open to see the root lying in two pieces on the dirt floor, Olivia still standing over me, her eyes huge, the hatchet raised.

I held up both my hands. "No more chopping!" I yelled, and then scrambled to my feet just in case she panicked and thought I was still being held.

My ankle was bruised and aching, but I hobbled over to the pile of stuff Liv had dumped out of Garrett's bag. In addition to the hatchet, he'd brought a disposable camera, some rope, and . . .

I picked up one of the plastic bottles, reading the label. "Hedge Hammer?" It was herbicide, a plant killer, and he'd brought three bottles of it.

Garrett might have chickened out, but at least he'd come prepared before that.

Except that we weren't dealing with a killer tree after all—not exactly—but ghosts *inside* the tree.

Was it still worth a shot?

I remembered how Rebecca and Octavia had felt in my head, that anger and frustration at the unfairness of it all.

Their spirits trapped in the tree where they'd died. If we killed the tree, would that release them?

Grabbing another one of the bottles, I tossed it to Liv. "Here!" I yelled, even as she ducked out of the way as the roots on the ceiling writhed and reached.

Liv caught the bottle, then frowned at it. "Plant killer?"

"Their spirits are trapped inside the tree, and the tree is growing inside the house," I told her. "It can't hurt!"

For a second, I actually thought Liv was going to argue with me that she didn't want to kill any plants.

Then one of the roots touched her hair, and with a shriek,

Liv whirled around and started splashing Hedge Hammer like it was her job.

I did the same, pouring out the other two bottles onto the floor, which was still rolling and cracking like there was a minor earthquake going on.

When the last bottle was empty, I tossed it, grabbing my bag with one hand and Liv's hand with the other, pulling her toward the stairs and out of the cellar.

CHAPTER 34

OLIVIA

We ran down the hill, arms at our sides, our breath sawing in and out of our lungs. My backpack flopped heavily against my back, and I was going so fast that the distant, sane part of my brain begged me to slow down before I tripped and rolled all the way down to our bikes.

But the other part—the part that knew it had escaped something super dangerous—begged me to keep going as fast as I could.

There was a grunt from behind me, and I didn't even have time to slow down or turn around before Ruby was careening into me. We went down on the grass hard, the breath leaving my lungs in a painful whoosh.

Something stung my knee, and I felt my elbow collide with something soft. Given Ruby's sudden cry, I figured it had been her stomach. For a moment, there was just the grass, the occasional collision, and the taste of my own sweat in my mouth as we rolled halfway down the hill.

And then I managed to dig my heels in and stop falling, Ruby coming to a stop around the same time.

We lay there in the grass, panting up at the starry sky.

"Ow," Ruby said weakly, and I pushed up onto my elbows to look over at her.

"Are you okay?" I asked. She was flat on her back, her arms spread wide, her eyes squeezed shut.

Glancing down, I could see the welt around her ankle. It had been red in the glare of the flashlight, but out here in the near dark, it was an angry bluish purple, and I thought again about the . . . thing wrapped around her, how close I'd come to not getting to her in time.

"Ruby?" I asked, rising all the way up and flipping around so that I was hovering over her. I went up on my knees and grabbed her shoulder. "Ruby?"

"I told you I liked 'Rubik's Cube' now," she said faintly, and then one of her eyes opened. "Also, no, I'm not okay, but I'm not dead? So I'll settle for not okay."

I didn't know whether I should laugh or cry, so I ended up doing some weird combination of both, a gurgly, snotty sound that would've been embarrassing if it had happened in front of anyone besides my best friend.

With a groan, Ruby sat up, wincing as she touched the dark band around her ankle. "That part was very not cool," she muttered, then twisted to look over her shoulder at the house.

It sat there in the moonlight, looking a lot creepier than it had that first day, and whether that was because it was dark or because we now knew exactly what was inside of it, I wasn't sure.

"Do you think it worked?" she asked, and I sat back on my heels, looking.

There was nothing, no sign of what had happened in the house. It sat there as still and silent as ever, just a house.

"I don't—" I said, and before I could finish, a loud *CRACK!* split the air. The ground underneath us rumbled, and as I watched in horror, the earth began to open up at the base of the giant oak tree, a long split snaking from its trunk and racing downhill.

For us.

"The tree!" I yelled, and Ruby shot to her feet even though it must have hurt her ankle.

"I hate trees so much now!" she yelled in reply, and then we were running again, stumbling and loping to the bottom of the hill, the whole ground shaking beneath us like we were in the middle of an earthquake.

"Oh man oh man oh man," Ruby was muttering, and there were more sounds behind us, the cracking of wood, the rumbling of the earth, and underneath it all, a high-pitched sound almost like shrieking.

My foot smacked hard on the packed dirt of the road, Ruby right behind me, and only once we were off the grass did I finally stop to look back.

There was a fissure running from the base of the tree nearly to the edge of the lawn, one thick root shooting out of it, the tip sharp. Like the roots in the cellar, it moved in a snakelike way, swaying back and forth, and I honestly felt like I might throw up.

"It's not long enough," Ruby said next to me, her breath coming back. "It can't catch us, it's not long enough."

And sure enough, the root was moving and twisting,

stabbing up at the sky, but we were too far away. Still, watching it *reach* for us had me grabbing Ruby's arm and pulling her back even farther until we were on the other side of the road.

It wasn't just the oak tree's root that was moving, though. The ground still shook, and the whole tree swayed like it was being pushed by strong winds, leaves falling off in masses, fluttering to the ground. The low rumble felt louder now, the shaking harder, and the tree groaned and shrieked, the root still straining for us as we stood there, frozen, our chests moving with the force of our breath. Ruby was still holding on to me, favoring her unhurt ankle, and her fingers gripped my wrist.

"Liv," she said. "The house."

But I already saw it. Like the tree, the house was starting to shake and move slightly. There was the bright, sharp sound of glass breaking, and as we watched, the windowpanes tumbled out of their frames, crashing onto the porch.

And then one of the massive columns holding up the veranda started to tilt.

"That seems not good," Ruby said, and before I could reply, the column crashed onto its side, the veranda coming down with it.

It was all so loud that I cringed, actually putting my arm up in front of my face as a gust of wind blew over us, smelling like old wood, dust, and that same sickly-sweet smell from the cellar.

After that, everything happened really fast.

The ground around the house continued to shake and shudder even though the road where we stood was perfectly still except for the vibrations coming from up the hill.

The house was cracking and quaking, the area around where it stood shifting and sinking.

"It's going to fall," I said, almost wonderingly, and Ruby shot me a look even as she tried to balance on one foot, taking weight off her ankle.

"Um, yeah," she said. "It's already fall—"

And then anything she could've said was swallowed up in the loudest sound I had ever heard. It was a mix of more of that cracking, plus creaking and groaning, like the house or the earth around it was actually in pain.

The shaking got stronger, rattling my teeth, making it hard to stand up, and as Ruby and I watched, the ground opened up, tufts of grass shooting up into the air.

There was more groaning, and so much dust and debris that it was like a tornado was coming through.

The giant oak outside made a sound like thunder as it crashed to the ground, the jolt making me and Ruby both shriek and jump back so that we nearly stumbled into the tall grass lining the other side of the road.

The house sank into the ground as though a large hand underneath were pulling it down. Within a few heartbeats, all I could see was the top floor, the attic window where I'd seen that shadow. The attic where Ruby and I had been trapped. And then that was sinking beneath a lip of earth, too, and there was nothing but a giant hole and the felled oak tree.

Then, almost like an afterthought, that tree started sliding backward until it had vanished into the hole as well.

One more shudder, a deep one, like the ground itself was taking a really deep breath, and then . . .

It was the quickest thing. Later, I'd wonder if I'd seen it at all, or if all the craziness of the night had gotten to me. But I could swear I saw two figures in white, hazy and faint, holding hands and standing there just at the edge of the hole where the house had been. I actually opened my mouth like I was going to call out to them.

But as quickly as they'd appeared, they vanished.

The night was suddenly quiet and still, the only sound me and Ruby nearly hyperventilating as we stared at the hill where Live Oak House used to stand.

No surprise, it was Ruby who spoke first. "So . . . I mean . . . *technically* we did not do that."

The laugh started as a rumble in my chest, and then suddenly I was nearly cackling, throwing my head back as I laughed and laughed, tears running down my cheeks.

Ruby looked over at me, the most serious I'd ever seen her.

"Have you cracked?" she asked. "Did the house make you go crazy?"

Still unable to talk, I shook my head, wiping my face. I thought of the days we'd spent cleaning in there, all of our plans, my insistence that we not do anything that might damage the house.

Well, *that* clearly hadn't worked out.

"We are so totally Bad Kids now," I managed to gasp out to Ruby, and she shook her head, snorting.

"Cracked," she muttered, then began limping down the road toward our bikes. I wasn't sure if she'd be able to ride or not, but she climbed on with only a little grimace.

"So now what?" Ruby asked, maneuvering her bike into position.

I glanced back at the empty hill, wondering what anyone would say when they came here and found Live Oak House vanished.

"We go home," I finally said. "And never worry about writing down how many chairs are in one room again."

That made Ruby snort again. "This was a lot of work just to get out of summer camp."

I laughed at that. I kind of couldn't help it. And then we pedaled away from what used to be Live Oak House.

Neither of us looked back.

CHAPTER 35

RUBY

Walking into the rec center the next morning—okay, limping, really—was one of the weirder experiences of my life.

And since I'd almost been eaten by a tree, I figured that was saying something.

Mom was next to me, her whole body drawn up stiff, lips pursed together, and I dared a glance up at her. "Still mad?" I asked, and she looked down at me with her eyebrows raised.

"Do you really need to ask that?"

I didn't.

So our plan to sneak back home last night had not exactly worked out. The sneaking *out* had been easy enough, but no one ever tells you it's the coming *back* that's the tricky part. Mom had caught me halfway through my window, and even though I'd been able to convince her that me and Liv had just decided to ride our bikes around town, I was looking at being grounded for the next decade, probably.

"I can't believe you'd do something so reckless," Mom went on as we made our way toward the gym. She normally just dropped me off in front, but last night's shenanigans meant that I now had a full-time escort keeping an eye on me at all times. "I mean, I *can*," Mom corrected, "but I can't believe you got Olivia to go along with it."

"We were fine," I insisted, and Mom gave me a pointed look. I'd told her I'd hurt my ankle falling off my bike, and now I held up my hands, acknowledging that I wasn't 100 percent fine. "It was one little fall—"

"And if you'd been alone, think how bad that could've been!" Mom said, and I had to admit that yes, she had a point there.

But honestly, Mom being mad at me—and she had plenty of reasons to be mad at me—was the least of my worries that morning. Had someone already been out to the house? Did Mrs. Freely know what had happened? And if she did, would she suspect me and Liv had anything to do with it? What if Garrett spilled the whole thing? Ugh, I should've known not to trust him, I should've asked Susanna, she probably would've been a better choice. I made a decision right then and there to choose my partners in crime more *carefully* in the future.

We walked into the gym, and I knew immediately that what had happened at Live Oak House was not a secret.

Okay, maybe the part we played in it was, but from the way Mrs. Freely was darting around, talking to a group of really not-happy-seeming adults, it was clear that everyone knew Live Oak House was toast.

Mom walked over to the group that included Liv's mom, and I trailed behind her, just in time to hear Mrs. Willingham ask, "What do you mean, *gone*?"

Mrs. Freely stood there, her hands opening and closing at her side, her eyes big. "It's . . . gone. The entire structure collapsed in on itself. The fire department thinks it must have been a sinkhole."

Mom folded her arms over her chest, tilting her head down. Mrs. Freely did not know that look, but I did, and it meant Mom was about to go off.

Since that going-off would not be directed at me, I have to say, I was a little excited to see what might happen.

Liv's mom came to stand next to mine. "Apparently, they think it was some kind of sinkhole?"

Her tone made it pretty clear how she felt about that, and I realized for the first time that Liv kind of sounded like her mom.

"A *sinkhole*?" Mom repeated, her voice climbing up the words as her eyebrows rose.

Mrs. Freely looked nervous for the first time since I'd met her. "W-well," she said, only stammering over the word a little, "that's what it seems to be. Which is of course very strange given that the house has stood there for over a hundred years and there's never been a sinkhole in town before, but—"

"How could that happen?" Mom asked, and I did my best to keep my face very still. The other kids were watching us, and I met Liv's eyes for a second. Hers were wide, her face kind of pale, and next to her, I saw Garrett frown.

As Mrs. Freely kept stuttering out excuses about the house being perfectly safe as far as anyone could know, I gave Garrett a significant look and just managed to keep from drawing my finger across my throat so he'd get the hint. We were not about to get ratted out by the guy who had been too scared to even go into the house with us the night before.

But Garrett gave me a nod and a thumbs-up, his hair flopping over his forehead like it did, and I realized that while Garrett might be kind of a coward, he was still loyal, apparently.

Maybe that crush could happen again after all.

When my gaze slid back to Liv, she was watching me with a smirk that was so uncalled for, and if my mom had not been standing right in front of me, I might have given her a hand gesture that let her know exactly how I felt about being smirked at. Instead, I stuck my tongue out, which just made her grin.

In real life, friends were so annoying.

RubyToozday: You know one good thing about everything at Live Oak House?

OliviaAnneWillingham: If you say something mushy about us becoming friends, I'm going to log off.

RubyToozday: Gross, no.

RubyToozday: Also, why did you change your name back?

RubyToozday: Actually NVM, I like this one better. More YOU.

RubyToozday: BUT ANYWAY. No, the one good thing is not our new bestiedom, soon to be confirmed with necklaces and MAYBE matching tattoos.

OliviaAnneWillingham: Ruby.

RubyToozday: MAAAAAYBE.

RubyToozday: It's that A) we learned we're SO GREAT that even GHOSTS want to be our friends and keep us in their spooky house forever and evvvvvver, AND B) thanks to Rebecca and Octavia Wrexhall, we now know that you and Emma are NOT the weirdest pair of twins ever.

OliviaAnneWillingham: Ugh, don't say that. What if they're not gone and it makes them mad or something?

RubyToozday: They're totally gone. We destroyed their tree AND their house.

RubyToozday: But you don't think keeping their doll was a bad idea, do you?

OliviaAnneWillingham: Ruby, I swear . . .

RubyToozday: JOKING JOKING, like I'd take anything from that house of horrors. No, everything Live Oak House is gone, including the ghosts.

RubyToozday: And now you and Emma actually seem normal.

RubyToozday: That was the point I wanted to make.

OliviaAnneWillingham: You know, I think we ARE normal now. Me and Em. Or normaler?

OliviaAnneWillingham: Which is not a word. Anyway, she's coming home on Friday.

RubyToozday: Nice.

OliviaAnneWillingham: And she wants to hang out Saturday, but I told her we made plans.

RubyToozday: Diiiiiid we have plans?

RubyToozday: Drawing a blank on plans.

OliviaAnneWillingham: No, but I thought we could now MAKE some.

RubyToozday: You are a sneaky gal, Liv, and I love it.

RubyToozday: YES. You, me, bookstore?

OliviaAnneWillingham: Sounds like a plan!

RubyToozday: And then, since we'll be generous, maybe Emma could meet us at Yo Yo Yo later?

OliviaAnneWillingham: And hang out? All three of us again?

RubyToozday: We could give it a try?

OliviaAnneWillingham: Yeah. Okay.

OliviaAnneWillingham: But I'm not getting the healthy yogurt.

RubyToozday: NO YOU ARE NOT. FRIENDS DON'T LET FRIENDS EAT HEALTHY YOGURT.

OliviaAnneWillingham: Okay, so see you Saturday, Rubik's Cube?

RubyToozday: See you then, Olivia Anne Willingham, Esquire.

ACKNOWLEDGMENTS

I feel like every time I sit down to write acknowledgments, I'm thanking the same people, which makes me feel very grateful indeed for the wonderful team I have working on these books! Ari Lewin, Holly Root, Amalia Frick, Elyse Marshall, Anna Jarzab, and Jen Besser, you are an incredible team of women, and I am so lucky to get to work with all of you. Thank you for everything you've done for me and my books!

Julia Brown and Meg Allen, you've both been on the receiving end of many "I THINK I FORGOT HOW TO BOOK" emails, and have always been there to make me laugh or remind me that I say this every time. Finding the two of you is proof that the internet may be dark and full of terrors, but it's also pretty magical.

Alison Goodman, Alwyn Hamilton, Sabaa Tahir, and April Tucholke, y'all were the best tour mates a girl could have, and had we not gone on "Penguin Teen on Detour" to the Winchester Mystery House, this book would not exist.

I'm always writing pretty great moms in my books, and that has to be because I'm lucky enough to have one myself. Thank you, Mama.

John and Will, as always, you're the MVPs of my life.

**TURN THE PAGE
FOR ANOTHER SPOOKY TALE OF
FRIENDSHIP AND ADVENTURE**

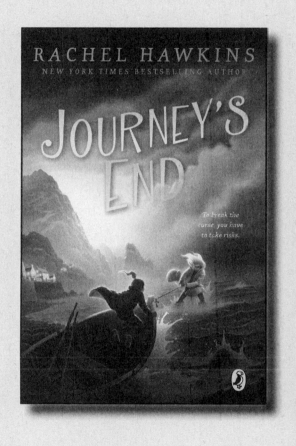

CHAPTER 1

ALBERT MACLEISH WOKE UP EARLY ON THE MORNING
he disappeared.

It had to be early if he was to leave without his mum
and da noticing, so it was still murky and dim when he
opened the front gate and slipped out into the quiet,
rutted lane that ran past his house. It had rained the night
before, and he was careful to keep from stepping in the
puddles that dotted the road. He'd dressed in the dark
that morning, and he'd been in a hurry, slipping on the
first pair of shoes he'd found. Unfortunately, those were
his good shoes, the ones he wore to church, and Mum
would hide him good if he got them dirty.

Moving gingerly, he skipped over one puddle, skirted
another. It was barely dawn, but as he passed the other
houses on the road, he could see people moving inside
them, shadows behind curtains. At the McLeods', his
friend Sean's father was already heading down the front
steps, fishing pole in hand.

"Morning, Bertie!" he called out, not seeing how Albert winced at the nickname. He'd always been a Bertie, but now that he was nearly thirteen, he'd decided it was high time he was called Albert. Too bad no one in Journey's End seemed to agree.

"Mornin', sir!" he called back. Sean's father was a bigger man than Albert's own da had been, with heavy feet that stomped into the lane, obliterating the little pools of water Albert had been so careful to avoid. As Mr. McLeod clomped closer, one giant foot sent up splatters of rain and mud, dotting Albert's trousers.

He winced again and Mr. McLeod clapped a beefy hand on his shoulder.

"Where you off to so early, lad?"

For a moment, Albert panicked. He hadn't thought to come up with an excuse should anyone see him heading toward the village. The MacLeishes were farmers, not fishermen, so unlike Tom Leslie or James McInnish, he'd have no reason to be down at the docks this time of morning. By all rights, he should be milking Maud or feeding the chickens.

But before he said anything, the front door of the Mc-Leods' swung open, Sean's mum standing there, a bucket dangling from her hand. She looked like Sean, all tiny features and wispy blond hair. "Yer lunch, Robert," she said, the corners of her mouth quirking so that Albert knew

2

this wasn't the first time she'd had to remind Mr. McLeod of something.

Albert used that as an opportunity to hurry on down the lane, and soon the McLeods, their cottage, and any questions they might ask about why a farming boy was walking out to the shore at this time of morning were far behind him.

As the road curved uphill, Albert moved faster, his breath coming out in small white clouds. The air always smelled of salt and sea, but that morning, Albert could also smell the very first beginnings of spring, a rich, loamy green smell that made him smile, and when he crested the hill, he began to whistle a bit.

Journey's End was nestled at the base of the hill, surrounded on its other two sides by rolling green. The sea pressed at its back, crashing against the high, rocky cliffs. There were houses on those cliffs, solid wooden structures that belonged to families much wealthier than Albert's. He'd always liked those houses, how stubbornly they clung to the top of the cliffs, big bay windows jutting out toward the ocean. They made Albert think of tough boys, their chests puffed out as though they were challenging the sea to just *try* to take them down.

Albert's older brother, Edward, had sworn he'd live in one of those houses someday. Edward was gone now, and while Albert liked the big houses on the cliffs, he had no intention of staying in this village when he was older. Sometimes he wondered why anyone did, and if he was the only one who thought there was something a little sad about being born in a place called Journey's End. It seemed like a place where people should end up, not where they started out. He'd tried to ask Edward once, but Edward had just ruffled Albert's hair and told him there were too many thoughts in his head.

He headed down the hill, the road turning from mud and puddles to cobblestones. Over in Wythe, the next village over, they had paved streets. But then, people in Wythe had automobiles, too, and no one in Journey's End—not even the people in the houses on the cliffs—could afford an automobile.

The sun was higher when Albert reached the village proper, and he could see Mrs. Collins opening the door to her shop. She waved at Albert as he passed, but thankfully didn't ask what he was about.

The docks were to his right, and Albert skirted those, turning instead to the left and the little trail that wound down to the beach. There wasn't much shoreline in Journey's End, and what existed was covered in sharp pebbles that Albert could feel even through his nice shoes.

He stood there, hands in his pockets, looking out at the water. A mile offshore, a wall of gray rose up from the water. It covered the sea below, climbing high enough to mingle with the clouds, and no one could have mistaken it for a regular fog bank. It was too solid, for one thing, never drifting or dissipating like fog usually did. The sun never burned off this wall of mist, which seemed as permanent as the rocks on the shore, as the cliffs that stretched over the sea.

But more than that, there was the feeling you got when you looked at what everyone in Journey's End was trying so hard not to talk about. Not that anyone could avoid talking about the fog for long, of course, but when they did, it was said in a whisper—*the fog*—that slid through people lips, then hung heavy in the air. Even now, Albert felt the hairs on the back of his neck stand up, and there was a sick kind of swirling in his stomach, the same he'd felt the day Edward had dared him to jump from the hayloft. He'd done it, but the twinge in his ankle reminded him what a foolish decision it had been.

He hoped this decision wasn't that stupid. Or painful.

For as long as Albert had been alive, the fog had clung to the rocky island where the lighthouse stood, like the island was a master keeping its beast—the fog—on a tight leash.

But sometime during the winter, the light had gone out. They hadn't been able to see it at first—the fog was too thick for that—but slowly, the gray had begun creeping closer, sliding across the waters of the Caillte Sea . . . slowly, but surely.

All his life, Albert had heard the legend of the lighthouse, that its light was what kept the fog at bay, but he'd never truly believed that. He wasn't sure anyone did. But as the fog slithered closer, so too did the story of its light, something to do with a witch and an ancient curse.

There was something else, too, something that Albert didn't really understand. When the fog had started its creep toward the land, some of the people in the village went to a meeting in the town hall—a meeting that was meant to be secret.

Edward had still been here then, and he and Albert had sneaked down to the hall, trying to watch through the cracks in the slats, but all they'd seen were some of the men from the village standing up, a tall, dark-haired girl in their midst, her face pale, her clothes odd.

"Did you put it out yourself?" Albert had heard a voice ask. He'd thought it was Mr. MacMillan, the man who owned the dry goods store in town, but he hadn't been able to see. "Is that why ye've come back?"

That was the part that had seemed so odd to Albert. Come back? From where? He was sure he'd never seen the girl before in his life, and near every face in Journey's End was known to him.

Their da had caught him and Edward then, and the hiding they'd both gotten had nearly driven the memory of the mysterious meeting from their minds.

Then Edward's friend Davey McKissick had taken a boat out to light the light himself.

Davey hadn't come back. Neither had Davey's father when he went looking for him.

And then Edward had declared that he'd light the light. The fog had seemed more dangerous by then, creeping close to shore, and more stories were told now, in louder voices. Stories about the fog sliding through the village, making ships and houses disappear. Warnings that if it came into the village, it would snatch people from their very beds.

More tales Albert had never really believed in, but looking out now, he could feel it, pressing in with curling fingers.

The waves were gentler here in the sheltered cove, but they still sent bursts of salt spray into the air as they crashed against the smaller boulders near the shore. Albert was a farm boy in his heart, and looking out at that gray water, he longed for mud underneath his shoes, for the sweet smell of hay in his nose.

But he knew this was the best chance he would have, and if he didn't start now, he would lose his nerve altogether.

Bending down, he removed his shoes, then his socks, setting both on a high, flat rock nearby, hoping that would keep them safe from the worst of the spray. Later, the group of men sent to look for Albert—Sean's da among them—would find his shoes. They would be all of him anyone would ever find, and his mum would keep them on the mantelpiece until the cold day in December 1928 when her broken heart finally stopped beating.

He hopped down the beach much the same way he'd hopped down the path to the sea, skirting rocks instead of pebbles, but his feet got scraped up anyway, the salt water making every step sting.

Over the years, the sea had carved hollows into the cliff side. Edward had said some of these caves went back for miles, turning into tunnels that ran underneath Journey's End, and that if you weren't careful, you could get lost forever underground. Albert hated those stories, and as he passed one of the bigger hollows in the rock, he shivered.

The cave Albert was looking for wasn't very deep at all. It went back only a few feet, but he still swallowed hard as he ducked inside the dark opening. Here, the sound of the sea was both louder and more distant, like putting his ear against a seashell, and Albert worked quickly, wanting to be out of the cave as quickly as possible.

The little rowboat hidden behind a shelf of rock had seen better days, and its hull (once painted blue, he thought) was now a faded and scratched gray. A handful of barnacles clung to the side, and the entire vessel smelled strongly of rotting fish, but Albert smiled as he tugged the boat out of its hiding place and toward the sea.

He had found it just a few days ago, not long after Edward had vanished into the fog. Even though the Bible said stealing was wrong, and Albert's mum and da would both have taken the strap to him, he told himself that it wasn't stealing. It was *finding*. Albert had kept his eyes peeled in the village for any signs announcing the loss of a rowboat, but there hadn't been any, and Albert had started to think of the little boat as his. The *Selkie*, it was called, the words painted in curling black script.

As he dragged the *Selkie* to the shallows, Albert's heart thudded in his chest and he tried very hard not to think that maybe the reason no one had reported it missing was because whomever it had belonged to was dead, lost out there beyond the fog bank.

The frigid water was lapping against Albert's ankles now, the boat thudding against his shins as he tried to steady it with one hand. The oars rested in the bottom of the boat, and they rattled as Albert climbed inside.

For a moment, he sat there on the splintered seat, the boat rocking but not yet being tugged out into the ocean. His breath was coming fast now, and not from dragging the boat. It was fear. But nestled right up next to that fear, as tight as the barnacles on the side of his stolen—*found*—boat, was hope. This would work.

It had to.

Albert lifted his eyes once more to the rolling bank of gray blotting out the horizon. Out there in the fog was a high, rocky crag. He couldn't see it now—the fog was too thick—but atop that crag was the lighthouse. Someone had lit it once, saving Journey's End, and Albert knew this was the only way. It had taken Davey McKissick and his da. It had taken Edward. But it would *not* take Albert. He wouldn't let it. Hadn't he found this boat just after Edward vanished? Wasn't that some kind of sign that he was meant to take it, and go after his brother?

He hoisted the oars, pushing off one of the nearby boulders. Behind him, Journey's End, the village he'd known all his life, the village that would one day put his picture on a wall with all the other sons and daughters, brothers and sisters, it had lost to the sea, receded into the fog.

And Albert rowed off and became a mystery.

FROM "THE SAD TALE OF CAIT MCINNISH,"
CHAPTER 13,
Legends of the North

CAIT HAD NEVER BELIEVED IN THE FAIRY STORIES.

If she had, neither she nor the boy might have died, but Cait was a sensible girl, and when she saw the old woman washing the boy's clothes in the stream, she had thought nothing of it. She and Rabbie were making their way back from the village, his hand small and warm in hers, and as they'd passed, Cait had simply thought the washerwoman must have had a grandson of her own, another bonny boy with a blue tunic marked with the stag of the laird's house.

Had she known her stories, she would've recognized the washerwoman as a Bean-Nighe, the fairy who came as an omen of death, washing the clothes of the doomed in streams and rivers, and it might have made her eyes sharper, her feet swifter.

Maybe later in the day, when they'd come back to the castle, she would've been fast enough to catch Rabbie when he ran past her, giggling, the sun shining on his copper-bright hair. Maybe her fingers would've caught his tunic (*blue, so blue, blue as his eyes, blue as the sky he was rushing to meet*). Maybe she would've caught him before he stumbled, arms spinning as he pitched toward the castle's open window.

Maybe, maybe, maybe.

Cait thought the word enough that it sounded like a spell itself, a constant chant in her mind.

But she did not catch him, and even though that morning she had not recognized the Bean-Nighe for what it was, the fairy's warning came true all the same.

If this were one of those fairy stories Cait did not believe, the boy might've sprouted wings that would have saved him at the last moment, when he'd gone soaring over the rocky cliff and icy sea. He would be revealed as a changeling, a fairy himself, blessed. Protected.

This is not one of those stories.

READ THIS SERIOUSLY FUN SERIES FROM *NEW YORK TIMES* BESTSELLING AUTHOR RACHEL HAWKINS!

★ "As surprising as it is delicious."
—*BCCB*, starred review

"If Buffy the Vampire Slayer were Southern instead
of SoCal, raised on good manners, Cotillion, and
sweet tea—she would be Harper Price."
—*Justine*

LOOK FOR RACHEL HAWKINS'S CHARMING ROYAL ROMANCE!

"Sweet, romantic, and adorable, fans of Meg Cabot
will thoroughly enjoy Hawkins's latest!"
—**BuzzFeed**

"Teens won't need to be fans of the royal gossip columns to
enjoy this light, funny take on the fairy-tale world of royalty."
—*School Library Journal*

"Lighthearted, pure fun."
—*RT Book Reviews*